"There we go," Tony said, putting a crowbar Matt had brought with him to good use on the locked porch door. With his extra weight and strength, the wooden frame of the door next to the lock broke, and the door juddered inwards. "Easy." He and Matt swapped weapons and moved inside the main nave area of the gloomy church. Grabbing the shotgun, Tony ventured two steps inside. There was a gap between wooden pews to his left, right and in front. He immediately saw that he was not alone; the church pews had lying, sitting figures dotted all around. Thirty or so his mind quickly calculated. Then he noticed the gait and movement of the figures as they began to rise and notice his presence. He saw the gnawed bones on the stone aisle leading up to the chancel and altar. Then, at last, his mind registered that the people inside who had become so interested in his intrusion were all faceless Infected.

THE
RED DEATH

BOOK 2 OF THE END OF ALL FLESH

BY PETER MARK MAY

THE

RED DEATH

BY PETER MACKMAY

The end of all flesh is come before me; for the earth is filled with violence against them; and behold I will destroy them with the earth.

Genesis 6:13

I love *The War of the Worlds* by H. G. Wells, the book, and musical audio drama, as it mentions Walton-on-Thames where I was born and the local area I knew so well. I always wanted to set something in real places, where local people could recognise and get the same thrill from as I did as a boy.

This is a fictional book, set in the real world, with a situation not beyond the stretch of the imagination. Nothing is scarier than that.

PMM

For Paul D.Voyce & Sarah Walker

CHAPTER ONE

STILL, NO HOPE

The group, weary, deflated, and soggy from the knees down looked around at each other, wondering what to do next. Woking had been their goal; now that too had been swept away by the Red Death and flood waters.

The group of survivors stared at each other, lost and bemused, until a single shot rang out to break the silence.

They all turned at once in fear towards the direction the shot had come from, but they could see no threat. The side window of the army vehicle was now cracked and a circular spray of visceral blood coated the insides. The Royal Artillery Captain had obviously taken the quick way out of his suffering.

It began to rain again, and everyone hurried under the shelter of the large roof that spread from the railway station main exit over to the nearby line of shops. Brita and Piers checked the area. The concrete planters seemed not to be hiding anymore unwanted Infected.

"What the hell are we going to do now?" Matt's voice was high and anxious as he flapped his arms up and down at his sides.

"Get the hell out of here and head south to Aldershot or Farnborough?" Ann repeated what the officer had said about the evacuation zones.

"They could end up like this place before we even get there," Selena said, peering out through the rain for any sign of living people or the Infected. No one spoke for a few seconds.

"Well I'm fucking going to that hotel," Ayesha suddenly said, wiping away her tears. "I'm going to find some new clothes, have a shower and eat my guts out and then worry about what to do next. I'm sick and tired of having crap clothes on, frizzy hair and cold, wet feet."

"Sounds good to me hun," Charlie said, backing her up with a hug.

"We could all do with getting dry and having food and beds to sleep on," Ellie agreed.

"Might as well." Even Tony sounded tired.

"Anyone know the way to this hotel?" Hannah asked.

"I do," Ayesha pointed from under the roofed area down the road they were on following the brick wall of the railway. "Let's get going eh."

Piers and Brita flanked her, with Charlie and Ellie and then the rest following after. They hadn't noticed the clouds catching up with them earlier, and all felt down-hearted as they moved out in the rain again. Hannah had a sudden urge to pee but hoped she could hold it until they reached the hotel or some-place to safely hole up for the night.

They passed some takeaways and other shops that seemed to have little use in the current climate. They hurried past a side road that led into the shopping heart of the town but spotted no one about as they did.

The group splashed on past a nail bar, estate agents, and a RSPCA Centre when they really needed an outdoors clothes shop and maybe a corner shop with bottled water and cans of protected goods. The road curved around from the high station walls, and Ayesha pointed to a tall building ahead and slightly hidden to the left of the road. "There's where we need to be."

They cut through a paved alley next to where a market was sometimes held, thus avoiding the main part of town. Over a crossing, there was a corner shop. The sandbagged door was kicked inwards, and the insides were dark and gloomy, but invitingly full of food.

"Supplies," Tony grunted and made a beeline for the shop, with Ann in tow. Her stomach was grumbling so badly; she would risk anything for a tube of *Jaffa Cakes* right now.

"What if it's not safe?" Hannah warned.

"That's breaking and entering and stealing what you are contemplating," Selena pointed out rubbing her side. She had a stitch from carrying the backpack; she did not feel like eating, but a drink of some sort would be most welcome.

"Fucking hell Judge Judy, who is going to frigging arrest me?" Tony boomed out his laughter as he entered the shop.

"You going in?" Piers asked Brita, who was the only one of them apart from him carrying a decent weapon.

"No," she simply said, with a curt shake of her head.

Piers looked at his axe and against his better judgement, followed the married couple inside. Ayesha followed Piers inside with a worried looking Charlie trailing after her. The rest of the group decided to stay outside under the ripped awning of another shop next door. The wait outside seemed to take ages, as the remainder of the group scanned the streets for any sign of life. The wide double lane roads in either direction were shielded by a large office block.

Hannah looked out at the rain again, wondering if they would ever get a break. She had hoped to be saved by the government, army or police, but it seemed once again that the group had to save itself. Her feet were numb, wet and ached like hell, she was hungry, sick and thirsty all at the same time and her urge to pee was becoming painful. Just as she thought she might piss her three-day old pants, the shop looters emerged with bags crammed full of goodies. Tony and Ann shared nothing, but Ayesha, Charlie, and Piers handed out a chocolate bar and bottle of water to each of them.

"Can we get going now, I need the toilet urgently," Hannah whined.

"I could do with the bog myself, little girl," Tony splashed past her, sending water up her nearest leg. Frowning she moved off, the pain in her full bladder easing a little as she began walking again. A left turn at a crossroads brought them to the glass-doored entrance of the hotel. An ambulance, an army truck, and two police vans were parked outside in a protective half square in front of the door. They had to squeeze through a gap, easy for most, but a right old kerfuffle for the Gables.

Piers and Hannah reached the double glass doors first. They were locked tight.

"I'm so going to piss myself in a minute," Hannah muttered as she rattled the locked doors.

"Good job you have a fireman handy, step back," Piers said to her hefting his axe, as Hannah moved to a safe distance. He was about to swing when a young woman with peroxide blonde hair and black eyebrows in a hotel staff uniform came rushing at the glass doors waving for Piers to stop his axe swing.

"No, no, no," she shouted through the glass in an Eastern European accent. "Stop, stop."

Piers let his axe drop.

He and Hannah, who were closest, noticed that her white blouse under her open purple waistcoat opened at the top to reveal a glimpse of a sky blue bra underneath. The badge on her left chest said: Zuzanna.

"Can you let us in please," Piers asked her politely through the glass.

The woman tucked and buttoned her blouse some more, as she was joined by a soldier buttoning up his combat jacket whilst fumbling with his rifle, much like the one Brita carried.

"I need to use the loos," Hannah shouted through the doors.

"Fuck off," the dark-skinned soldier with a black beret barked at them.

"Fucking let us in mate," Piers swore back.

"Don't be a cunt," Tony shouted over their heads, not making the situation any better.

"You might be bloody infected. What's wrong with her, like?" The soldier jabbed a finger at where Hannah was hopping from foot to foot to ease her near bursting bladder.

"I'm pregnant, and I need a fucking piss, mate!" she screamed at the gunner through the glass doors.

"I ain't your mate," he said back to her, taken aback at her screaming through the door at him. "You could be hiding the infection under your clothes?"

"You want me to fucking strip off then?" Hannah raged pulling off the ugly cardi Selena had given to her. Then she fumbled at the buttons of her jeans.

"What's she doing," the gunner said to his female companion.

"Taking clothes off, let them in Steve please, they look fine to me," She pleaded, rubbing the soldier's large arm.

"Your Captain Burton sent us here." Selena moved up to the top step, glad to be out of the water for a while.

"He's still alive?" the soldier looked less hostile.

"He was when we left him," Selena stated. Not exactly lying, but not exactly telling the full truth of their encounter. "He said you would take us in."

"You're a soldier, follow orders," Ayesha yelled from the back. The rain was making her shiver in the scrubs and lost property clothes she was wearing.

"Please," Hannah said in a softer voice, putting one open palm on the cool glass between them.

"Okay, but no fucking around, I'm in charge here," the soldier slung his weapon and fumbled for the locks at the top and bottom of the doors.

Everyone nodded quickly. Anything to get out of the cold rain and off the dangerous dead streets of Woking town. The group had to control themselves as they waited to bundle in through the one glass door the soldier opened. They all trooped into the lobby where two electric lamps were set up on the reception desk to their right. Further right was a Martian War Machine mural on the wall, from H. G. Wells's *War of the Worlds*. Directly ahead were lifts and a stairwell doorway and in-between that the reception desk. The lobby was well lit because of the glass door and side, but the corners looked gloomy.

"Where did you get that?" The soldier pointed at the same sort of rifle he carried only a slightly different type and colour.

"I'm Danish army," was all she replied leading Ellie into the centre of the reception area.

Soldier Steve watched as the rest of the group walked in-between them looking strangely garbed and bedraggled. He then went over and locked the doors again.

"I am Zuzanna, welcome to the Woking City Centre Premier Inn," she said repeating the welcome she had spoken a thousand times or more since she started working there after arriving from Poland. "We have no electricity, but the shower and hot water still work."

"Who are all you people?" Soldier Steve looked at the motley group. "And why are you dressed like that?"

"Most of us were evacuated from Kingston Hospital to a temporary military medical camp in Surbiton where we were given a clean bill of health. The place was sadly overrun by infected carriers of the disease or plague, whatever you want to call it, and we escaped along the railway tracks to here." Charlie stepped up to explain.

"Where we thought we'd be safe," Ayesha added.

"I don't think anyplace is that safe anymore luv," Soldier Steve said, shaking his head. "We were overrun too, Woking has fallen so I locked this place up the best I could."

"How many of you are here?" Selena asked.

"Two," Steve replied.

"Two soldiers, plus you two?" Ann asked hopefully.

"Just Zuzanna and me. Nobody else. The rest of my squad are either dead, infected or have gone AWOL. I'm Lance-Corporal Steve Wright by the way and not, as you can see by my skin tone, any relation to the old DJ."

The group did their own introductions, Tony jumping over Ellie to bellow at the soldier. "So *Soldier Boy*, what the fuck are you going to do now to take care of us?"

"Fucking hell mate, I let you in, my duty of care ends in this bloody lobby. All the doors to the rooms are open, so pick one you like, just avoid the top floor which is ours. A lot of the guests left in a hurry so if you search about you will find some dry clobber to put on."

"But you are the army?" Ann said, "you should give us a clue what to do, where is safe."

"Ain't you realised yet, the South-East of England has fallen to this Red Death plague. It's total Fubar out there. Most people die, but about ten percent turn into Ebola look-a-like killing machines. You can't reason with them, their sole aim is either to kill you or bite you and pass on the disease. The Government are hiding in bunkers under London, The Royals are in Scotland and the armed forces and civilian police who were cut to record low strength before this shitcake went down and are losing control. We—you, are on your own." Steve explained in easy to understand loud words.

"What about Aldershot and Farnborough?" Matt asked, remembering what the Infected Captain had told them.

"The army are evacuating all healthy people to Royal Navy ships at sea, military come first of course. The thing is, can you make it to one of those places before the Red Death hits hard? My orders were to hold the town until further orders. I have no officers or NCOs left, it's just me and Zuzanna, and we are going to hole up here until the disease burns itself out. We have enough food for months and plenty of supermarkets to procure supplies nearby. You can stay or go, it's your choice, but just don't bother us okay?" Steve put his arm around Zuzanna and led her over to the desk to grab a plastic lantern.

"What are we going to do?" Ellie asked Brita.

"Where are you going?" Tony bellowed at the soldier's back.

"I'm going to finish off the shag you interrupted, is what I'm going to do. What you do is your business. Just don't open any outside doors and we will be fine. Laters." Steve casually waved and walked up the stairwell with Zuzanna.

The group stood around the lobby, just looking at one another, not speaking a word. Surbiton had been a disaster, Woking had fallen, and their hopes of rescue and safety had evaporated like the sunny weather. The lobby was dry and warmish, but their wet clothes clung to their cold skin for the most part.

Selena let out an almighty sneeze to break the silence.

"Bless you," Hannah said first.

"We need to find rooms and get out of these damp clothes before we catch our deaths," Selena said.

"And find some bloody proper grub, I'm Hank Marvin," Tony said loudly.

"Let's go find some rooms then." Charlie pointed and then headed for the door.

"What about the lifts?" Ayesha ran over to push the nearest unlit button.

"No power, no lifts, bimbo," Tony informed her in his usual

cutting uncouth way. He grabbed Ann's hand and led, almost dragging her, pushing in front of Matt to get to the stairwell first.

The rest of the group let him go first, glad to see the back of him for a while.

"What a knob jockey," Ayesha said, meeting up with Charlie by the stairwell. Charlie counted to ten, to give the rather obese Gables a head start, and then followed them up the stairs.

CHAPTER TWO

THE HOTEL

Because of the layout, the rooms started on floor three and went up to nine. Tony and Ann Gable bailed on the third floor as they were out of breath and cramping up already. Hannah wondered to herself how they had even made it this far. She was pretty sure they had used up a year's worth of walking in their old lives in the past couple of days. *Might help shift some of that fat around their guts,* she thought wickedly to herself. *But, I'm not going to be exactly thin myself in the coming months,* she chided herself.

Matt hovered by the door to floor three, kept open by the toe of his shoe. He grabbed Hannah as she walked past. "You want to share a room for safety's sake?" He whispered, his eyes glancing up to see if Ellie had heard him.

"NO, I don't want to share a room with you now, or ever again. I shared your cock and look where that has gotten me." Hannah said extra loudly, and Matt let go his grip of her and hurried off shamefaced through the door onto the third floor to find a room alone.

"Good on ya sister," Ayesha whooped from further up the stairwell, and even Ellie flashed a quick smile at her. The rest of the group decided to stick together and made it to the seventh floor before aching backs and legs caused them to give up their ascent and find the nearest rooms each.

Piers went along opening each door with his axe first to make sure they were all vacant. All fifteen rooms on that floor were. Most were empty with made beds, some twins, but mostly doubles. Five of the rooms had been occupied, three had left suitcases full of clothes and personal items left behind in the rush to leave. Piers and Brita left the open suitcases out in the corridors for people to pick up clothes. All three suitcases had belonged to ladies, but Piers had his Fireman's gear on at least. Hannah picked a double room next to Selena while Piers took one across the hall from them. Ellie and Brita picked a double to share right at the far end of the corridor and Charlie and Ayesha a twin room two doors down from Piers.

Hannah, who at least was wearing her own clothes, took off her coat and trainers and opened a packet of shortbread biscuits to nibble on as she surveyed her closed but not locked hotel room. She heard a sneeze through the wall from Selena's room as she padded barefoot over to the window to fully pull the curtain open and let in as much natural light as possible. She knelt on the chaise long just under the cold window and looked out through the rain drop covered pane at Woking below. Her view was of trees and townhouses, and not much of the road or pavement could be seen. In a way, she was glad of that. She finished one biscuit and turned away from the window as she started the next. She missed the Infected little skinless girl staring up at her from behind the thick trunk of a sycamore tree.

She had never had a hotel room to herself before. She pushed open the bathroom door with her cold big left toe and peered inside. It was gloomy inside, but the shower looked so very inviting. It would be getting dark before she knew it, so decided it was time to get warm. The door to her room could be locked from the inside, so she flipped the catch and took off her top and flung it on the bed. It held on for a second and then joined her wet jeans, socks and wet trainers on the floor. She thought about picking it up, but holding her arms over her cold body, she headed inside to grab the free shower bottle and mini soap instead. She started up the shower and was surprised that it was warm enough. She plunged under the warm water letting her aches drain away. Her bladder painfully reminded her of the need to pee. She looked at the toilet next to her and then decided just to go in the shower. It felt wrong, but also good at the same time. She washed her body and hair and five minutes later was wrapped up in three different towels and under the duvet of the hotel bed. She was asleep before she even felt tired.

Brita and Ellie showered together. It was not sexual, just easier as the water was already cooling. Brita washed Ellie's hair first and then did her own. Brita made Ellie sit on the chair in front of the desk, which had a mirror in front of her. She dried and then combed her lover's hair with a brush they found in the luggage outside. Ayesha had already bagged the best clothes for her and Charlie before they had showered. Brita loved the fresh smell of Ellie's hair as she brushed it. They both stared at the plastic teapot next to them, wishing they could brew up coffee. They had new clothes and underwear each, but no bras in their size, but it was just good to be together, alone and out of the rain, and away from the death and flood waters outside.

Ellie volunteered to brush Brita's tangled mess of shorter almost white blonde hair. She was a minute in when thoughts of her dead parents caused her to break down in floods of tears once more. Brita took her to bed, and they just held each other skin-to-skin close, as Ellie sobbed into Brita's neck. Brita loved the physical contact from her lover, but the crying grated on her a little. She wasn't used to sharing such emotional outbursts with anyone. Her tears had always been hidden or sucked down deep until her throat hurt. Showing weakness as a child and then in the army just led to more pain and more abuse. She rubbed Ellie's back and prayed she would fall into an exhausted sleep soon. Then she could move over to sleep on her side of the bed.

Selena sneezed three times like some automatic rifle coming out of the warm shower into the cold air. The shower, change of clothes and biscuits had made her feel better for a while, but then she felt a tension headache coming on right behind the bridge of her nose. She had wanted to unpack her rucksack, but could not raise sufficient energy to do it. It sat, with its top flap open on a chair by the desk, looking like a monstrous egg from one of those Alien films. Selena sneezed again and lowered herself deeper into the thick duvet; maybe some sleep would make her feel better. Her tired mind was filled with dead ends, of her car hitting something over and over again. She had no one left to give herself up to it seemed, as her mind drifted off into lucid dreams and darker nightmares of the id.

Ann had to find another shower in another room, as Tony's large frame was hogging theirs. *Hers* was lukewarm at best, but she was glad to feel clean. She stayed in the other room as long as she dared. Finding two drawers of unpacked men's clothes. She found a large white shirt to put on and used a clean towel as some kind of skirt, fixed with a belt until she could find anything better. The dry socks on her feet were the most blessed thing she had felt in ages.

She was heading to see if she could find any other more suitable plus size clothes to fit her when Tony summoned her by name. She knew by bitter experience that only having babies and being in the bathroom were acceptable excuses to miss such a bellowed call from her husband. She made it back to their room, just stopping a second call. Tony stood large as life (or larger) toweling the remains of his hair, the rest of him damp and naked.

"Where's my clothes?" he grunted, showing his hairy arse as he wandered over to the bed.

"I haven't had time to search out all the rooms yet. If you weren't such a big old hunk of love, it would be easier to find togs for you to wear," she said with a faked tired smile.

Tony turned and sat on the bed, making it look like a single, his balls and flaccid, but still large penis almost winking at her. She went into the bathroom and picked up the dirty towels and mopped up the water on the floor with them.

"Sod doing that love, come here a second Annie," he said in a softer voice from the bedroom.

Ann's heart sank, and she wished she could dive down the shower plughole like some genie and disappear, but she had no escape and knew what was coming. Ann had only one chance of saving herself from his crushing missionary weight: distraction.

"I was going to wander down to the restaurant or kitchens to find us some grub, luv," she said, coming out of the bathroom folding towels and trying not to look at his now excited man parts.

"Ooh," Tony said scratching at his groin. "Good plan luv, off you toddle then. We have plenty of time for husband and wife stuff later."

"Okay," Ann said putting the towel on the bottom shelf of the open wardrobe. "Toodle-loo." Ann waited until she reached the stairs, before letting out a sigh of relief. She hoped nobody would be about to spot her in her strange garb. The idea of food had travelled swiftly down from her brain to her rumbling empty stomach.

"Yeah, and if there is any chocolate cake, it's all mine," she muttered to herself as she descended the cold stairwell.

After their showers, Charlie was lying on her twin bed, while Ayesha put on a fashion show wearing a sports bra and un-matching, but clean small panties she had found. She was smil-ing, dissing most of the unfashionable or old clothes she had gathered together, but at least they had shelter and something new and not scrubs and crocs to wear.

"This is frumpy looking, you can have that," Ayesha said tossing a brown sweater Charlie's way.

"Thanks, Ash," Charlie replied with a raise of her eyebrows. She was glad to see her adopted daughter smiling again, even if it was for a little while. "I could murder a cuppa."

"But the kettle don't work," Ayesha held out a white rose printed top and weighed up its fashion merits. "And it will be getting dark soon too."

"I could go down to the kitchen and see if the gas is still on and boil us some water, maybe cook us up dinner."

Ayesha tossed the blouse over to Charlie. "Now you're talking."

Charlie grabbed the blouse and put it on. She found some jeans that Ayesha had thrown her earlier and started to get dressed. "Thought you might like that idea."

"You can do that, and I can ask Piers if he would like to join us for dinner and maybe afters." She winked at Charlie.

Charlie shook her head and pulled on some socks and some

trainers she found in her size. "I'll knock before I come back in shall I?"

"Good plan," Ayesha smiled back at her.

"If you leave the room, don't shut the door, or we might not be able to get back in, or put the latch on if you can." Charlie gave her a quick passing hug and then left the room.

Ayesha could not find anything the least bit seductive, so walked up to Piers' room in only her undies. Her knock brought Piers and his impressive six pack to the doorway wearing only a towel.

"You look erm...lovely," he slightly stammered at the flesh on show.

"And you are overdressed babes," Ayesha said, walking in and reaching for his towel.

Matt sat alone in his third-floor room, wondering how only last week he had two hot sexy girls to fulfil his sexual fantasies, And now he was alone in a darkening room, with only rolled up toilet paper for company.

"Maybe we should go round the table and vote what we would like to do," Charlie suggested. "I think we should stay, for the time being at least."

"Seems fair," Piers added. "Stay here."

"Staying put," Ayesha began.

"Same," Hannah said raising her hand like she was back in school.

"Stay." Ellie squeezed Brita's hand under the conference table.

"I'm staying with Ellie," Brita said.

"Going to Aldershot to get away from you tossers," Tony stated in his usual tactful way.

All eyes on the table were suddenly on Ann. She never craved the spotlight, not even on her wedding day. She wanted to stay, but could not defy Tony, he was her husband, until death do us part. "Going," she said sadly.

Only Matt was left. He looked around the table, looking at Hannah and Ellie giving him evils. He liked the safety of the hotel, but he could see the hate in both his ex lovers' eyes. "I'm going." He regretted his words as soon as he spoke them, but he couldn't go back on them without looking spineless.

"Well, that's sorted then," Steve said standing up. "Take as much supplies as you can carry. I've got a map you could have to show the route to both evacuations points."

"Cheers," Ann nodded at him.

"Hey, where's the posh bird?" Tony said realising that they were one short around the conference table.

"She's not feeling well at the moment," Ayesha said without thinking.

"Is she infected?" Steve asked the group.

"No, no, we think she is ill because of all the crud in the flood water," Charlie explained quickly.

"You fucking sure? If she's got it, then we are all up shit creek." Tony stated bluntly. "Ann get our stuff; Matt go get some supplies from the kitchens. Soldier man, show me this map of yours, we are leaving as of now!"

"Zuzanna, fetch this man the map I showed you the other day," Steve said kissing her cheek. "I think I better see your ill friend for myself and assess the situation and dangers."

Charlie and Hannah did not like the fact that Steve grabbed his assault rifle from where it leant up against a low cupboard before following the staying group upstairs. Ann went with them but left the group at her floor. Nobody wished her luck or goodbye. Alone and scared for what the outside world might throw at them again, Ann cried a little, and she packed what little they had into bin liners she had found earlier on a maids' trolley. She hoped Tony was making the right choice, and not some bloody-minded decision to leave people he disliked, and get them all killed in the process.

CHAPTER SIX

NOT SO, FOND FAREWELLS

Hannah led the way up to Selena's room.

Ellie stopped Brita at the rear of the group on the stairs. "Look we don't all have to go trooping up there, why don't I fetch us some food and water."

Brita stopped and scanned her lover's face. "It's okay if you want to say farewell to Matt, you were engaged, and this could be the last time you see him," Brita said, her face deadpan and unreadable.

"I love you," Ellie said, putting both her fingertips on Brita's face before kissing her.

"This is good to know, now go before I change my mind and become all butch lesbian on your behind."

"You can go all dominant later." Ellie winked and then waved. "This won't take long."

Brita smiled as best as her tight mouth muscles would allow. She wasn't happy at all, but she had to trust hers and Ellie's love somehow. She frowned, forming ugly lines across her pale forehead and then continued upstairs after the others.

Hannah opened the door, and Charlie and Steve slowly entered the room. Selena lay tucked up to her neck in the bed, she appeared to be sleeping. A bin lay next to the bed, and the room smelt foul from her recent sickness and diarrhea. Steve's hand absently moved to his nose and mouth as Charlie moved over to the bed. The rest of the group loitered outside, so as not to crowd the sick woman's room, or that's what they told themselves.

"Selena, we're back, how are you feeling?"

Selena didn't move or reply.

A cold feeling rose from Hannah's feet to her stomach, *was Selena dead?*

"You said she was just sick, not infected," Soldier Steve stated.

"I'm still alive thank you, just sick as a dog, young man," Selena said, turning and opening her eyes slowly.

"How are you feeling?" Hannah raced forward two steps and then stopped in fear for her unborn child, if Selena was infected.

"I guess the army is here to check me for red sores." Selena flung the duvet back to reveal her pale, but unblemished naked form underneath.

Steve had a good look and then turned and left the room without a word. Selena looked milky white all over and a bit thin, but she had no signs of the infection on her. Charlie rushed forwards to cover her up, but Selena waved her away and leant over the side of the bed to vomit in the hotel bin.

Charlie grabbed some tissues from a box on the desk at the end of the bed and hurried round to hand them to Selena when she had finished.

"Water, please," she gasped wiping the bile from her lips and chin.

Hannah rushed over with a fresh strawberry flavoured water she had brought up with her, and Selena took it as she rolled back into bed. Charlie emptied the bin in the bathroom and then washed it out.

"You should not be in here in your condition, Hannah," Selena said, propping herself up on her pillow and taking a sip of water.

"I wanted to see that you are alright?"

"Well, you've seen what I am like, you best run along young lady," Selena said closing her eyes and breathing through her nose. "In fact, it's better if everyone leaves me alone until this bug has run its course. So bugger off, for now, maybe come back later with some toast."

"You sound on the mend already, dishing out menu orders," Charlie said.

"Out, please, I want to be sick in private if you don't mind," Selena said in her cruelest of judge voices.

"Come on." Charlie ushered Hannah from the room. "We'll be back later with toast then." She pulled the door after her. Hannah looked at Charlie, feeling a little upset at Selena's terse words. "Don't worry, she's ill and proud, and cranky. I'll grab you later, and we'll take her some toast, okay?"

"Okay," Hannah nodded.

"What we gonna do now?" Ayesha asked, her eyes flicking to Piers' tall,, handsome frame. She had a few ideas to while away the hours.

"Where's the soldier boy?" Charlie peered around the rest of the group to find him gone.

"Gone to see the fat couple and the baby daddy off," Ayesha replied without thinking. She turned to Hannah. "Sorry mate."

"Glad to see the back of him," Hannah said and headed off to her room. Glad, wasn't the right word, as her feelings were mixed. She hated Matt, but also, he was the only person she really knew that well from her old life. It would be easier for her, Ellie, and Brita with him gone, but that didn't stop her crying into her pillow about his impending departure either.

"We need to prepare, if we are staying here for the duration," Piers said to the rest of the group in the hallway.

"Like what?" Ayesha asked moving closer to him.

"Well, light for when it gets dark. Candles, torches etcetera. Maybe we should coordinate with Steve and see what he wants us to do. We need to make this place secure as possible, but have at least two escape routes too."

"Let's go find Soldier Steve then," Ayesha said putting her arm through Piers' before dragging him off to the stairwell.

Charlie raised her eyebrows, as she and the rest of the remaining group followed after.

"Hey, for you," Ellie rushed into the lobby with a large bottle of water outstretched in her hand towards Matt.

He and the Gables turned away from the door as she ran over. Zuzanna was at the open hotel doorway, and Steve outside making sure the coast was clear.

"Thanks," he said accepting the water from her. "I didn't

expect you to come and say goodbye after all that has gone on." Matt looked down at his trainers.

"Well, stuff happens in life. Not always as we planned."

"I don't have to go?" Matt gently put his hands on her arms and led her away from prying ears.

"But you do," Ellie said with steely resolve. "I'm with Brita now, and the stuff with Hannah is just too weird for you to stay. Be safe out there, though." Ellie leant in and kissed his cheek before fleeing upstairs.

Matt touched his wet cheek and felt a wall of misery come crashing down on him.

"Come on soppybollocks, we ain't got all day waiting for you to sort your love life out." Tony's mocking tones brought him back to the reality of life again. He trudged after the Gables who had not waited for him and left the hotel.

He saw Steve walk back in, no words of luck were exchanged. The soldier and Zuzanna locked the door after him. Holding a rucksack of food and heavy water he followed after Tony and Ann, hoping this was the right thing to do.

"I need some proper clothes and outdoors camping gear before we leave. So we will have a look around the shops and see what we can find. I'm fucking sick of having cold, wet plates of meat."

Matt nodded and trailed after the married couple into the cold, murky flood waters again.

Ellie met the others on the stairs coming the other way.

"Is Steve down there?" Piers asked her.

"Yeah. The others have just left," Ellie stopped and moved to let everyone but Brita pass.

"So, you okay?"

"I am now," Ellie replied and crushed her lover in a tight embrace. "What are you lot up to?"

"Seeing what the soldier wants us to do and find candles for tonight."

Ann hated the choice of leaving the hotel even more. They had headed over the crossroad and into the town centre towards the shopping centre there. The road dipped as it went along, which was okay for Tony and Matt, but she was up to her waist in oily cold water. Tony had to drag her along as they made for the Peacock Centre's nearest entrance.

Ahead and to the right was a raised area out of the water with a pavilion. To Ann's relief, Tony helped her towards it. Not for her sake, but to get a better view of their surroundings. Matt waded after him, not taking in his surroundings. He was trying to figure out how his life had got so messed up in such a short period of time.

Ann's relief of being out of the water did not last long. A double scream of a woman or a child echoed around the area from close by. Tony dragged both her and Matt into a crouch behind a bench with a low brick wall and with two trees at their right to aid their concealment.

A woman in her thirties with brown hair trailing behind came into view, carrying a toddler in her arms. She was running from the flooded centre area towards them when ten Infected splashed out from a shop entrance to encircle her and her boy. She screamed at the top of her lungs, but it only brought twenty more Infected people that had been chasing her.

Before Ann, Tony or Matt could think or blink they were on her dragging her and her child under water as they surrounded her like a rugby scrum. Ann hid her face into Tony's arm as they ripped the mother and child to pieces.

"We need to get out of here now," Tony hissed. Keeping low the three of them retreated back to the steps down into the water again, when some of the Infected lost interest and began rampaging through the waters around to where they were retreating. They would be exposed any second!

"Here you are?" Zuzanna handed out T-lights and matchboxes to the female members of the group. "Not exactly perfect, but all we have."

Everyone was on the third floor, apart from Hannah and Selena. Piers and Steve were blocking the rear stairs with beds, sofas; filling the stairwell so no one could get through in a hurry. The main stairs they used filing cabinets from the manager's office to make a narrow space so only one could pass at a time. The gap they blocked with three doors from unused rooms, slid in the gap on top of each other between the four upstanding filing cabinets on two sets of steps. The cabinets were lashed to the banisters with rope. They made a similar moveable obstruction at the top of the stairs on the third floor, giving a defendable position against attack from below.

"Will this keep them out long?" Piers asked heaving another door into place.

"For a while," Steve stood up and exhaled. "We will block this stairwell from above on the fourth and fifth floors and use the rear stairs to move up and down to here. The restaurant has good line of sight on the road below, so we should post a watch every night from here. I've got two sets of night vision goggles we can use. Lights only to be used behind pulled curtains after dark."

"Like the blitz," Piers remarked.

"Yeah like the blitz," Steve nodded and wiped sweat from his brow.

"Do you have any more weapons?" Piers pointed at the assault rifle leaning up next to a fire extinguisher.

"Yeah, but they are army property mate," Steve said, eyeing the fireman up and down.

"Oh," Piers said sounding disappointed.

"I'll keep the situation under review. If I think the danger levels rise, or the threat of imminent attack is likely, I'll show you how to use them, and only then."

"How will you know?"

"Oh, I'll bloody know alright. Come on, let's go block the next floors up with beds now."

Tony grabbed Matt and Ann's collars and dragged them behind the cover of a partially submerged L-Shaped hedge, just before the wild splashing Infected creatures glanced their way. Ann felt the flood water cover her crouching legs and behind. *Her hotel donned clothes were wet and ruined already.* Her hand went to her mouth to stifle an anxious giggle that wanted to escape. The three of them were in extreme danger, and nothing in her terrified state was amusing. *Maybe I'm losing it.*

Tony's big left hand found her and gave her the gentlest of squeezes. Her eyes flicked up and over to his stern face, as she did not want to move and attract the Infected people's attention. He was worried, yes, but had no real fear on his big stupid look-ing old face. She just wished he could be this man more than the default ogre he usually was. Her whole body was tensed, mak-ing her calves and the back of her thighs ache as she crouched.

Ann held her breath as the splashing grew closer to their position. She waited for the awful cry of discovery that would spell their end. She couldn't outrun a toddler let alone them, she knew that much. That made her think of Maddy and Jayden. Her breath was burning in her lungs, and the edges of her vision were growing cloudy.

One of the Infected was right on the other side of the hedge they crouched behind.

CHAPTER SEVEN

RETREAT

Brita, Ellie, and Ayesha were helping Piers and Steve block up the rest of the stairwells so they had places to fall back too if they were overrun. Brita was the most help, Ellie tried her best, but Ayesha just made a token effort while eyeing up Piers' muscular biceps.

Charlie and Zuzanna were cooking up something hot for them to all eat at lunchtime. Hannah checked on Selena, but she was sleeping, so she did not want to disturb her. Alone, she wandered around the hotel. Sometimes in tears about her sister, while sometimes swearing under her breath with seething anger. In her weakest moments of forlorn despair, she even wanted to be back in Matt's arms again, but those moments did not last long.

Hannah found herself up on the seventh floor, in an empty room overlooking the deeper flooded parts of Woking. Past the edges of the town was a common, the high parts of it had become an archipelago of green islands in a brown sea of death. She perched on the gloss painted windowsill and leant her head against the cold glass and stared at it for ages.

Ann felt like she might keel over and faint. Only the thought of falling back and maybe swallowing the sewer mixed flood waters kept her aching knees and ankles locked solid.

A high-pitched painful, mournful cry rang out from further away and immediately the Infected person by the hedge and the rest nearby splashed off back the way they had originally come. Ann exhaled and breathed hard in relief.

Matt popped his head up and down quickly like a Meerkat. "They're leaving," he whispered.

"We wait a minute and head back past the hotel and out of town," Tony said, rubbing his hands on the dry parts of his trousers.

Matt and Ann looked at each other crestfallen. They thought they might be going back to the dry hotel, but it seemed Big Tony was still intent on leaving. A minute of hearing only retreating diminishing splashes, Tony popped his head up to look around.

"They've gone. Come on it's time for us to leg it." Tony stood up in a crouch, which was normal size for most people. Matt and then Ann timidly stood up. Her left knee was burning white-hot while the rest of her lower, wet half felt freezing cold. The Infected people had left. She looked away quickly from the two corpses floating in their own sea of red. Tony helped her down from the raised hedge bed and into the deeper water. Hugging the left-hand pavement, they retreated slowly the way that they had first come.

They had reached the middle of the crossroads when a small group of Infected appeared near the raised pavilion area. Their screeching high-pitched cries of rage were the signal that the Gables and Matt had been spotted. Ann, Tony, and Matt began to run as fast as the waters would allow.

"Where we going?" Ann cried out in fear.

"Back to the bloody hotel woman, now shut up and peg it."

Hannah leant back from the window, leaving a greasy smudge from her teenage forehead. She felt hungry again and thirsty and wondered if that was due to the pregnancy already. She went to move off the windowsill as a wave of pins and needles hit her left buttock and thigh. She was dancing a jig and rubbing her bum when she saw them.

Matt, Tony, and Ann rushing through the flood waters as fast as they were able, back towards the hotel. Behind them, a group of five manic looking Infected were chasing after them. She rubbed her leg ready to move when she spotted another group far behind the first group of Infected. This group looked fifty strong, and their faces even from so far up and away looked ghastly. Hannah ran from the room, her numb bum soon coming back to life as she pelted down the stairwell, around and down as fast as her feet could take her. She got down to the fourth-floor level to find most of the remaining group and the soldier blocking the way down with beds and chairs.

"The others are coming back, the Red Death people are chasing them," she blurted out.

"What?" Steve asked.

"Calm down, Hannah, what's going on?" Ellie asked reaching out to grab the teen's gesticulating hands.

"Matt and the others are running back to the hotel, with shitloads of those manky Infected people chasing them," Hannah panted, easier to understand this time.

"How many?" Steve grabbed his rifle and made for the fourth-floor exit.

"Hundreds."

"Come on," Steve barked, and they all followed him through the door to race to the back stairwell. They had to use that to get down to the third floor and then back again to the front stairwell and moveable barricades. Even the super fit Piers and Steve were blowing hard by the time they made it to the upper third floor barricade. Brita was okay, but the rest of the women were in varying states of pain due to lack of fitness.

Piers, Steve, and Brita began to lift up the first two door barricades, while the others caught their breaths.

By the time they had reached the vehicle blockade around the entrance to the hotel, Ann's lungs felt like they might leap out of her throat and strangle her. Only Tony dragging her under her armpit was keeping her up. Matt squeezed through the gaps between vehicles with ease. Ann pushed herself through, hurting her thighs, belly and bottom as she did. Tony almost pushed the car in front forward, even with its brakes on to get through. Ann followed Matt up the steps and out of the water. He was banging on the glass and yelling for help at the top of his voice. Ann glanced back, but could see little as her husband's imposing frame was blocking the way. She reached the glass doors and banged on them, before peering inside.

The reception area was deserted.

Ann spun round just as the first of the wide bulging eyed Infected reached the gap they had squeezed through.

They were well and truly trapped.

They left the last door in position and jumped over it, Ellie felt better, so raced after Brita and the two men down to do the same to the lower barricade. Hannah, who had run the furthest and Ayesha, who was scared and slightly faking her knackered state, stayed at the top of the stairs. They had only lifted the first part of the lower barricade when they heard Matt yelling, and Ann suddenly scream from outside.

Everyone inside froze for an instant, and then quickly redoubled their efforts.

Ann screamed as the Infected ran at her. Apart from its vague shape and the torn dirty dress that clung to it, it was hard to tell what sex it was without facial features and hairstyles.

Tony grabbed the skinny Infected woman by the neck off her feet, and out of the water. Then grabbing its left leg, hefted it up and threw it back over the bonnet of the nearest car in the barricade. She bounced once leaving a ruddy stain on the silver paintwork of the car and then was gone from sight. Tony rushed to the larger gap he had made between the car and ambulance as another bulkier Infected person came running through. This one had an expensive business suit on and Tony roared and punched him in the throat sending him gasping for air and under the ankle high flood waters. Tony stomped on the man's head once, and he did not rise from his watery grave. An Infected soldier appeared in the gap, with a black beret on his head, with scalp and hair hanging down from underneath. Tony grabbed the back of his neck and smashed his face into the back of the ambulance three times hard, breaking every bone in the Infected soldier's face. Tony let the soldier drop blocking the gap a little at least.

Ann looked on in awe at the brutal fighting skills of her husband and what he was doing to keep her safe. He punched and kicked another to the water. When his back was turned, another Infected man appeared on the bonnet of the car.

"Tony look out!"

The warning was too late the Infected man had leapt onto the huge man's back. His big arms had trouble reaching around to shake the thing off. Ann looked at Matt, who was cowering in fear next to her. He was no help. So she ran down into the water again and grabbed the slimy ankles of the man on her husband's back and pulled him backwards with all her might. The Infected man lost his grip on Tony's neck, and his face planted hard onto the second paved step up to the hotel and stopped moving.

Tony gave her a broad smile of pride and thanks and a thumbs up. They retreated back up the stairs with looks of contempt for Matt.

"Oh shit," Matt said.

Ann and Tony looked around to see that the vehicles were surrounded by Infected on all sides and at least two deep. They were all diseased and their skin in varying degrees of rotting off their living flesh. With faces full of agonised pain, yet devoid of any human features. Eyes were wide, bulging and lidless; ears and noses taken by the ravages of the Red Death. The infection that did not kill them, but turned them into a living nightmare of a sub-species: driven mad by pain and the desire to kill or infect those who were not like them.

Ann could see the primal predatory lust in the Infected's wide eyes as they clambered onto cars and filled every possible escape route there was. She did the only brave thing she could and closed her eyes. She tried to picture all her lost family and grandchildren in her mind's eye; as they had been and not how they had become. She heard the scrape of hands and feet over the vehicle blockage and waited for death.

Ann Gable felt a rush of air across her left-hand side and braced herself for the painful end.

Someone grabbed her from behind and not in front. Her eyes flew open in shock and saw that Brita and Piers were dragging her back inside the small lobby of the hotel. Their gunfire exploded everywhere, the sound echoing off every wall. She looked back to see if Tony was okay. He and Matt were inside the glass door, as Steve stood firing into the Infected while retreating backwards into the lobby. She saw five or so go down, which made the others hesitate. It gave Matt and Tony time to close and lock the door. The rest of the Infected mob was soon at the doors, hammering and bashing their bloody fists, feet, and heads against the tough glass.

"Let's get back upstairs now!" Steve ordered. He covered their retreat his weapon moving left and right at the targets trying to break into the hotel.

Ann hurried past a set of filing cabinets at the bottom of the stairs. She hurried up as fast as her lungs would allow. Hannah and Ayesha grabbed her arms and helped her flagging body up through another new barricade that had been erected since they had left. She turned to see Tony and Matt helping each other slide three doors in the thin gaps between the filing cabinets while Steve covered them. With that job done they retreated up the stairs and did the same to the next barricade.

"Only two doors on this one," Steve said, "I need to see if anything comes up the stairwell."

"Come and get some food, water, and dry clothes," Ellie kindly said, leading Ann's aching body from the stairwell to the restaurant.

Ann just nodded and let Ellie and Ayesha lead her away to find some more clean clothes.

CHAPTER EIGHT

TRAPPED

The reunited group ate together in near silence. Steve and Zuzanna took theirs by the second barricade. The Infected were still outside banging on the glass and showing no signs of leaving. The doors and side window panels around the hotel's ground floor were holding for now.

Brita and a very twitchy Ellie took over the watch an hour later. Hannah watched the Infected from the window on the top floor of the hotel. She had a handheld radio, which she could talk to Brita or Steve if the situation changed dramatically down below. He had praised her to the hilt for spotting the danger and saving the others' lives. She was his *top eagle-eyed lookout*, and she felt a small burn of pride in her chest. It also got her away from Matt and the awful Gable couple he had thrown in with.

After an hour of being alone, apart from the odd radio message from far below, she became bored. Her mind began to wander and think about her passionate times with Matt.

"Lowlife scum cheating engaged perverted teacher," she verbally reminded herself aloud. The Infected were still trying to find a way in, they obviously had a lower boredom threshold than a pregnant teenage girl. She wandered from her side of the building to the next and the next trying to see any possible escape routes. Because they were well and truly trapped here, unless the Infected changed their tune and wandered off.

The area around the side of the hotel from the lobby gave little hope of escape nor did the back. Both were just sheer drops into a road or rear car park. The other side of the hotel gave the slightest means of escape. There was a two storey building about seven feet to the side of the hotel over a wooden fence. If there were windows that faced it on the third floor, they might be able to fashion a bridge across it and escape at night down the back and out of the hell Woking had become.

"Steve," she spoke into her handheld radio, "I'm coming down."

"Roger that," Steve replied. "Anything happening?"

"Nope, but I'm checking out a possible exit plan. Over," Hannah said, trying to sound all military and organised.

"Copy that," he said back.

Hannah took the rear stairs of the building. They ran down the side that the low-level building was, and she peeked at it at every turn in the stairwell that faced its way. The third-floor stairwell window was the last on that side that matched up with the low business building below. There were no floors below, just an open way on stilts that let the cars pass out through from the rear car park. The window was about a metre higher than the roof of the business below, but she was sure Soldier Steve could come up with a way of bridging that gap. Pleased with herself, she went to find him.

Brita and Ellie were holding each other close while they stood overlooking the second barricade. It wasn't ideal in Brita's mind, but Ellie was scared of the Infected banging on the glass in the lobby. Even she feared the sudden sound of shattering glass and what that would bring. So Ellie was a pleasant distraction. She had the British assault rifle with her, and Steve had left extra rounds of ammo behind. She could see the relief in his eyes that he had someone else to share the burden of guarding the hotel.

"What are we going to do when this is all over?" Ellie asked her after twelve or so minutes of silence between them.

"Depends if this will ever be all over?"

"Don't say that, I need something to look forward too."

"Sorry."

"So what would you like to do and happen between us?" Ellie kissed her cheek and tried to cling on to her old confident self.

"I would like to take you back home with me and find a cottage where we could be alone, possibly surrounded by land-mines and those rivers you have around your English castles," Brita said, twirling her right forefinger.

"Moats."

"That is it."

"Apart from the cottage, it doesn't sound too romantic."

"Ah, but I did not mention the queen sized bed and the huge hot tub and the reindeer," Brita smirked and then her thin lips and high cheekbones took on a more serious look. "And you would be my life partner forever in love?"

"Are you asking me to marry you?" Ellie said, raising her eyebrows.

"For sure, if you want to marry me," Brita said, feeling a red heat of embarrassment on her cheeks.

"I'm new to this all women thing, would I be the wife or would you be the wife?"

"It doesn't matter about labels and titles, as long as we are together, Ellie." Brita's cold blue eyes stared directly into Ellies'.

Ellie kissed her hard and passionately and the Infected below and their dire situation were forgotten for its duration. With the world falling apart around her, Brita felt happier than any other time in her life that she could recall.

Selena awoke to find that the clouds had rolled in again and most of the day had passed her by. Charlie had brought her some bread and crackers to munch at lunchtime and her empty stomach made her feel ravenous.

Selena sat up in bed, waiting for the waves of nausea that thankfully did not arrive. She was hungry, though, and feeling a little sick because of it. She ate the remaining one, and a half cracker left and then nibbled on the dry, slightly stale bread. It left her feeling dry, so she chugged down half a bottle of water, before realising this could be a bad idea. She waited in bed for five more minutes, but nothing came back up. She spotted a packet of two shortbreads on the desk opposite. Selena decided *enough was enough, time to get out of bed and stand on my own two feet.*

She pulled back the heavy duvet, surprised that it made her wrist ache. Someone had put a pair of knickers on her, for which she was grateful, she supposed. She checked out her feet; legs, tummy and chest for red blotches, but apart from her skin looking even paler than normal she seemed fine. She swung her legs out of the bed and touched the floor with her toes. There appeared to be an icy breeze encircling her bed and was glad to spot her rucksack on the chair next to the desk, which had clean clothes and socks in.

Selena pushed herself up from the bed with her arms. She stood, her legs buckled, and she sat back down with a light bump, where she had started off.

"Okay," she said to herself. "And once more unto the breach my friends, once more."

This time, her wobbling legs held her up. But she turned and shuffled sidewards, using her hands to push along the bed. She reached the desk and clung on for dear life. She grabbed the biscuits and tossed them onto the bed. They bounced once high, and Selena had a sudden fear that they would go on the floor, but they didn't. Then grabbing her heavy rucksack, she made a dive for the double bed with it. She collapsed on the bed with an amused giggle. A pair of socks and a spray deodorant rolled out of the rucksack, but it was all good.

Selena pulled on her socks first over her cold feet. David always told her she had terrible circulation. Then tucked into the shortbreads, not caring where the crumbs fell on the bed. Pulling on a pair of fresh, dry jeans was a bit more of a bum shuffle and palaver, but feeling tired, not sick, and fully dressed was well worth expending all her energy on. Thinking that was enough for the time being, she sprayed her stinking and hairy pits and pulled the duvet back over her. Another forty winks and she would be ready to face the world, or at least eat some of it.

Ann had left Tony below and had found a new fresh room on the seventh floor this time. A search of the once occupied rooms brought some new clothes and even a possible pair of big tall jeans that might fit her hubby, which was a bit of a miracle. She

washed her legs quickly in the shower as the water was freezing. She peed and changed her tampon and pad. Then washed
her hands and face in the sink. She stared at the gloomy haggard
reflection in the mirror. Ann pulled at the brown bags under
her eyes. She looked thinner in the face, and her love handles
and bingo wings seemed less wobbly than before.

"The Red Death diet, see the pounds fall off," she said to her
reflection. She went to smile, then thought of the skinless form
of Jayden running around Kingston Hospital, and she began to
cry. It took a very long time for her tears of grief to stop again.

Ayesha sat at the booth table in the dining area, eating a huge
bar of chocolate. She didn't care about getting spots and with
the lack of food and the sexercise she had been getting, she was
sure it wouldn't affect her weight. Everyone seemed busy or
were talking about what to do next, but all she wanted to do
was stay in the hotel, safe and sound with Piers as her bed-
buddy. She wasn't designed for outdoors; camping trips, lack of
food and she missed Facebook like fuck.

It wasn't like she was lazy, she did a hard day's work at the
salon, but she just wasn't cut out for emergencies and DIY, that's
what men were for, buying her stuff, fixing stuff and fucking.
She'd never painted her room, or changed a light bulb; she left
that to her two mums. She was their little princess, and that was
her role in life. She could see no role in this hotel, she couldn't
fight, cook very well or contribute. Ayesha felt lonely in a way,
at least she still had Charlie and Piers to care for her. She made
a good cheerleader, not a good sportswoman. She popped
another square of chocolate in her mouth and tried not to spoil
her eye shadow when she thought of her mother. She failed mis-
erably and went back to the safety of her room to wash her face
and reapply it.

CHAPTER NINE

THE GLASS SHATTERS

"See, what do you think?" Hannah pointed through the rear stairwell window to the two storey building below.

"I think I picked my eagle-eyed scout well," Steve said, and then spoilt all the adult pride Hannah was feeling by rubbing her head like she was some toddler who just named all her cutlery correctly for the first time.

Hannah stepped back from the condescending soldier just as an almighty smash was heard somewhere beneath them. Steve readied his rifle as the sound of breaking glass was replaced by the sounds of people hurrying about inside the hotel. They ran to the small stairs that led up to the mezzanine second floor. The stairwell was blocked high with beds, mattresses, chairs and a table. Yet, through the gaps, they could see a crowd of Infected trying to pull it all down, with their livid red hands. Steve took aim through one such gap and fired off a shot. A scream of pain ensured that she knew he had found his mark, but they could not see the infected person fall.

"Will it hold?" Hannah looked on anxiously as some of the barricades were pulled down from below.

"For a little while, but not forever. We better put your plan into action. Go tell Brita she might be getting unwelcome visitors. Then gather everyone else together here with food, supplies and get Piers to fetch two single beds and all the blankets we can find. Go, go." Steve urged.

Hannah hurried off up to the third floor just as Piers with

his axe, led Ann, Tony, Matt, Zuzanna and Charlie down the stairs to meet her.

"What's going on?" Piers asked anxiously.

"Are they in?" Ann called from the back of the group.

"Yes," Hannah nodded furiously. "Steve wants you to fetch two single beds and all the blankets you can carry to the third floor rear stairwell," Hannah said, racing on past him.

"Why?" He asked, bemused at the request unless it was to bolster the defences.

"Where are you off too?" Charlie asked her as she ran past.

Hannah looked back, confused and too focused on her urgent mission to know what to say. "Just fetch those beds. Steve will explain why. I've got to talk to Brita."

Charlie grabbed Hannah's hand to physically stop her this time. "Ayesha is up in our room."

Hannah looked at the pleading face of a parent and nodded. "I'll fetch her and Selena down."

Charlie pulled her into a tender, but brief hug and whispered in her ear. "Thank you. You will make a great mum."

Hannah just turned and ran through the doors and across the restaurant area. She was choked up, by Charlie's maternal words. But she had to swallow down her tears and emotions, she had a job to do. She was breathing fast by the time she reached a worried-looking Ellie and Brita. Their barricade and stairs seemed to be free from Infected incursions so far.

"We heard the glass breaking but haven't seen anything. Do you know what is going on down there?" Brita asked Hannah as she caught her breath.

"They've broken in near the rear stairwell. We, *no I* have a plan of escape. Stay here until you hear from me or Steve on the walkie-talkie. Then high-tail it over to the third floor rear stairwell." Hannah said, shaking her handheld radio at Brita and Ellie.

"How are we going to escape this place, there are Infected all around the building and inside now," Ellie said in a wavering, panicky voice.

"We are going to go over them," Hannah smiled back. "Look,

I've got to go, get Ayesha and Selena, okay? Just be ready." Then she was off again back out the stairwell door and racing to let Selena and Ayesha know what was happening.

"We should go now," Ellie said to Brita biting at the middle of her top lip.

"We are safe for the moment," Brita said, patting the assault rifle. "I will never let anything or anybody hurt you, my love."

Ellie faked a smile for Brita. Brita squeezed her hand quickly and then focused her attention on the stairwell. Nothing was moving or could be heard down by the first barricade yet.

She looked over at her Ellie, staring down the same stairwell, biting her nails.

"Why don't you watch the stairwell door for me?" Brita smiled at her.

"What, for those things?" Ellie paced, from side to side now, like she was doing a soundless dance at a club.

"No, because they can't get in. I want you to look out for Hannah or the others and hold the radio." Brita lied, holding the handheld radio out to her lover.

"Okay." Ellie nodded and took the radio and went over to open the door a crack and peer out.

Brita watched her for as many seconds as she dared. Ellie needed to pull herself together and grasp how dangerous the situation was that they were in, or she would get them both killed. Brita had an image of herself standing over a cowering Ellie while she battled a thousand infected that encircled them. She shook her head and blanked out everything but the first barricade.

"Can you walk?"

Selena was roughly awakened by being shaken. Her eyes felt glued together, and she had to rub them to focus on a worried looking Hannah bending over her.

"Can you walk?" Hannah repeated.

"Of course, I can walk young lady, I'm not a bloody invalid," Selena bit back a little too tersely, having being woken from a Patrick Swayze sex dream.

"Well get up then, cos the Infected have broken in," Hannah

shouted back, before moving over to help pack Selena's things. "Are you dressed?"

"For all occasions," Selena said flinging back the covers. She got out of bed and somehow kept her feet, even though a light summer's breeze might knock her over.

"What is happening and what are we doing about it?" Selena asked coming around the bed. She felt like she should be in a geriatric home at the moment, not attempting to escape murderous infected people.

"The Infected have broken in by the rear stairwell. Steve will hold them off, and I have come up with a plan to get us all out of here safely." Hannah clicked Selena's backpack shut and then handed her boots to wear.

"I knew you were the sharpest tool in the gene pool," Selena said, recalling something David used to say to her in Uni. She had a sudden overwhelming urge to find her ex-husband. Not to get him back, or spoil his new life, but just to say sorry for turning into the bitch she sometimes was. She had pushed away his love in favour of her career. With the world going to ruin, what bonus payment you got last review or what position you held meant nothing.

"Let's get going," Hannah said, nearly tottering backwards from grabbing Selena's backpack. The schoolgirl moved forward to take Selena's left arm.

"I can walk, it might not be fifth gear for a day or so, but I can move up my own locomotion, thank you, Hannah," Selena said proudly, as she walked stiffly towards the open door.

"What about your boots?"

Selena stared down at the boots she was carrying. "One thing at a time dear." She turned towards the stairs, but Hannah went the other way. Selena had to stop and turn like the QEII.

"You keep going, I've got to fetch Ayesha. I'll catch you up," Hannah called back.

Within a second, Selena thought. With Hannah not looking, Selena used the left-hand wall to help keep herself upwards. The stairs, well she would rise to that challenge when she got to it. But first, she needed to get her boots on.

Ann covered her ears as Piers smashed the toughened safety glass window on the third-floor stairwell. She had stayed at the window, while Charlie, Piers, Zuzanna and her husband had brought down two single beds. Zuzanna had fetched some tools from the handyman's store cupboard. Tony was drilling holes to bolt and then brace them together with spare bits of broken up tables and chairs to make it into a bridge to reach over to the roof of the business below.

Ann could see most of the others getting across, but she and Tony: well she could only picture falling and death in her near future. It was only when the botched bridge was placed on the windowsill did they see their error. The single beds were far too wide to fit in the glass-free frame.

"What are we going to do now?" Ann wailed as rapid rifle shots came in quick bursts from Steve below, making her jump like a scared cat on Bonfire Night.

"Fuck!" Tony exclaimed and kicked the beds he had spent ages bridging together. He had not noticed either, not helping his mood.

"I dunno," Piers said running his left hand through his hair in desperation.

"You're a fucking fireman, think of something," Tony shouted at him, unhelpfully.

"We need a ladder really."

"Do you have a ladder somewhere?" Charlie asked Zuzanna.

"No," the Polish hotel worker said, shaking her head.

"Maybe you could pop back to sodding Warsaw and pick one up for us, luv, bloody foreigners." Ann could see that Tony was winding himself up into a rage because he hadn't spotted his error with the beds either.

"Wait, wait, wait," Zuzanna said not hearing, or choosing to ignore, Tony's barbed words. "I went on roof once for a smoke. There was a ladder there, long one just left lying on floor."

"Can you show me where?" Piers came round to stand in front of the hotel worker.

"Yes, yes," she nodded in relief. "Follow me."

"Whatever you are going to do, do it faster," Steve shouted

up from below before he fired again.

Ann watched as Piers and Zuzanna raced off up the stairwell and then looked over at Tony. Everyone was giving him a wide berth as he prowled around the crowded stairwell like an angry bear awakened too soon from hibernation. Finally, he snapped, kicking the two beds to pieces and threw them all out of the broken window.

Ann let him do it. He was letting off steam, and he'd soon calm down once he had knackered himself out.

Ayesha was on the loo with her jeans and bikini briefs around her ankles, when Hannah burst through her hotel door carrying Selena's bulky rucksack.

They exchanged a brief and embarrassed look as Hannah turned to face the wall.

"Sorry mate," Hannah apologised with a long whistle.

"What do you want?" Ayesha wiped, pulled and flushed.

"The Infected have got in, but Steve is keeping them at bay, but we need to leave this place. Gather all your shit together."

"Oh fuck, really." Ayesha was more annoyed than scared at the moment. The hotel had been warm and had beds, food, and her fuck-buddy Piers. The thought of being out in the wet outside world again made her shiver all over. "How long do I have to get ready?"

"Ready?" Hannah asked her quizzically.

"Yeah, I've got to put my make up on, pack my clothes and beauty products I've found."

"Are you for real?"

"What?"

"Infected are trying to break down the barricades and come and kill us all, and you are wondering what shoes go with your top?" Hannah shouted at her.

"Okay, okay, no need to lose ya rag, girlfriend. So, five minutes to pack?" Ayesha pouted.

"Thirty seconds and I'm out that door and down the back stairwell without you, *girlfriend*."

Ayesha stared at the girl only a couple of years younger than her and then moved deliberately slowly over to the desk to pick up her brush and other girly home comforts she had found. She had hardly packed two items by the time Hannah had stamped, turned and left her to it. Alone in her room, panic and fear crept in, and she raced around the room stuffing all hers and some of Charlie's things into two matching black holdalls she had found. She ran and caught up with Hannah and Selena only half a floor down. They exchanged a quick sparring look, and then both helped Selena conquer the long trip down the rear stairwell.

CHAPTER TEN

SNAKES AND LADDERS?

"Where are you going?" Hannah called out to Piers and Zuzanna as they ran up the stairs as she and Ayesha helped Selena come down.

"Bridge didn't work," Piers said without stopping and carried on around the next bend. "After a ladder."

"Okay," Hannah shouted after his and Zuzanna's echoing feet on the stairs above.

"So much for your great escape plan," Ayesha said, slyly.

"Shut up."

"Ladies, please," Selena said, in a low warning voice that had her judge's edge to it. It did the trick, though. The two teen girls just glared at each other, over the back of Selena's neck.

The third floor was in panicky chaos by the time they got down there. Automatic weapons fire was still coming up from Steve a floor below. The window was completely broken out, and bits of bed debris and tools littered the floor surrounding it. Tony was sitting on a step down to the mezzanine floor, with Ann sitting next to him. Charlie was so pleased to see Ayesha; she gave her a hearty hug. Then she turned to Selena. "How are you feeling now?"

"Less terrible than before," she managed to say through a strained smile.

Hannah put down the older woman's backpack by the window and Ayesha, once out of Charlie's embrace, put down her holdalls there too. Hannah smiled hopefully at her and was rewarded with a grin back. Times were tense and scary, they were bound to bite at each other now and again.

"How are things going down there?" Hannah asked Matt, who was standing in the corner like an ex invited to the love-of-his-life's wedding.

"They are slowly breaking through," Matt said, but he looked glad that Hannah made him feel part of the group.

"There are hundreds of the buggers now," Ann stated from her step.

"Any word from Brita and Ellie?" Hannah asked, but her words were drowned out by a crashing noise coming down the stairwell at a rate of knots. Everyone jumped and turned to see what was coming.

Brita and Ellie had their own problems. The Infected had found their way around to the lobby area, and half of the first barricade had been easily pulled down. Only Brita's dead-eye shots were keeping them at bay.

Brita thought they must retain a little primal fear as they did not all rush at her at once. They had seen three of their fellow Infected shot and seemed to be working like a pack of rabid animals. Two more chanced their arm, Brita fired once into the chest of the first one, it went flying backwards, knocking the one behind it down also. This made the others wary again and hover around the edges of the staircase.

"Check the radio, see what is going on?" Brita shouted back at Ellie, who was cowering against the frame of the open stairwell door.

"O-kay," Ellie replied shakily.

An Infected popped its repulsive head around the corner and stared at Brita with its big lidless eyes. Brita fired, her shot hit the wall sending bits of plaster in to the Infected's face, making it dart back behind cover. She only had one more magazine left, they had to move sometime soon.

"This is Ellie, we are under attack, is the escape route ready yet, can we leave here now please?" Ellie let the button go but got only static in reply.

"Try again."

"Okay. This is Ellie, what's going on, what do you want us

to do the monsters are at the first barricade, and I don't think we can keep them back for long." Again, Ellie let the button go, but still no word came from Steve or Hannah. Then the sound of a crash jumped from the radio, and a faint voice cried out in the background.

"Look out below!" Piers shouted down the stairwell after a set of metal ladders slid down the steps and crashed into the far wall. Everyone moved over to the stairs as Piers and Zuzanna came rushing down to grab the double ladder again.

"Sorry," It slipped out of our hands; very heavy," Zuzanna apologised.

"Had to carry it down from the roof, I need a hand to extend and lock it in place before we slide it out the window. Tony, Matt, Ann, and Charlie all ran to help, while Hannah and Ayesha helped Selena get out of the way.

"What was that?" Ellie's worried voice crackled from Hannah's walkie-talkie.

"Just our escape bridge arriving. Nothing to worry about, get ready to move in a minute; over," Hannah replied.

"Okay, but don't be long," Ellie replied.

"Okay." Hannah let the walkie-talkie drop to her side, as the ladder was extended fully down the stairs. It wasn't too wide and was long enough to reach across with acres to spare. An immediate problem flashed into Hannah's mind, and an instant solution shot back.

"Here, hold this." Hannah pushed the walkie-talkie into Ayesha's hands and exited through the stairwell door into the restaurant area.

"Where the hell are you going?" Ayesha called after her, but the door swung shut before she could hear a reply, even if there was one to hear.

Selena watched Hannah disappear out of the exit but was too feeble feeling to go after her. All she could do was watch most of the group guide the ladder through the window and down to the roof of the business below.

Everyone that helped looked pleased with their efforts.

Yet Selena spotted one problem. The ladder was sloping down out of the window, so their end of the ladder was high up and pointing to the ceiling and would be hard for even the fittest youngster among them to scramble on.

"How are we going to get up on there?" Selena stated the obvious for the less mentally endowed in the group.

"With these." Hannah huffed and puffed her way out of the restaurant carrying two dining chairs to use as step ladders on either side of the bridging ladder.

"Brightest broach in the jewelry box," Selena stated and smiled at her chosen prodigy.

Charlie grabbed one of the chairs from Hannah, and they placed them either side of the ladder as Piers was tying off the ladder to secure it in place. The firing below intensified.

"Who goes first?" Matt said, edging towards the ladder.

"Women and children first mate, and that means you on both counts." Selena raised her eyebrows in shock at Tony's words, he was pointing directly at Hannah. "A child having a child, and it was your idea so hurry up."

Hannah looked at Tony and then around at everyone else in the group until she fixed her gaze on Piers. "It's all safe and secure. I'll help you up," he said to her.

Grabbing his outstretched arm, she stood up on the chair and then clambered up onto the metal ladder. It vibrated up and down a little as she got on, seeing this, Piers held the end of the ladder to stop most of the wobbling.

"Wish me luck," she said looking behind her at the group, especially Selena.

"Good luck," Ayesha offered waving the handheld radio at her.

"Get a fucking move on," Tony urged in his more usual manner.

Hannah nodded and started to crawl through the window. The rigid rungs on the ladder were so painful on her knees she thought she might cry. Then she was fully outside, looking down at a couple of Infected below that had not noticed her. She froze suddenly, knowing that if she fell, she and her baby would be dead in seconds.

"You can do this, think female Indiana Jones," she muttered to herself. Then the pain in her knees caused a change of tactics. She placed her trainers on the outside of the ladder along with her hands. This lifted her knees off the painful metal rungs, and she began to haul herself across the ladder with ease. Focusing on the grey, flat roof opposite, she was across the gap between the buildings and clambering off the other side in no time.

She rubbed at her knees and waved for the next person to come across.

Brita fired again three times killing two of the Infected, but not before they had brought down the bottom barrier. Nothing was blocking them from an assault on her position.

"We got to go," Ellie shouted from behind her.

Brita knew she had limited ammo left, and if they all ran at her, she would be overwhelmed. Ellie was right, they had to go now and just hope that the escape route was ready. Brita fired once more, making an Infected dance back behind cover as her round hit the polished wood flooring. She pulled the bed frame that leant up against the wall next to the second barrier down with a bang and hurried after Ellie through the fire door. Another bed frame was leaning next to it, and she brought that down too, and they both ran through the restaurant towards the rear stairwell.

The radio in Ellie's hand crackled, and a voice came through, but they were too busy running for their lives to worry about it.

"Selena, you next." Piers waved her towards the ladder.

"No, send the younger women first." Selena had no right to go before anyone else. If anyone deserves to go last and possibly getting caught by the invading Infected, it should be her. Her life to save others seemed appropriate, an eye for an eye.

"We ain't got time for your lady muck crap, now get on the ladder," Ann shouted at her. The fear was making the poor woman angry and overwrought.

Selena wandered over to the chair by Piers and the ladder and reached for her backpack. "Don't be stupid, I'll take that," he said to her as he offered her his hand.

Seeing that she was holding up a very nervous line, she climbed up onto the ladder. Feeling clammy she gripped the ladder carefully and with gritted teeth went through the window. Once outside she made the mistake of looking down, and a wave of vertigo nearly made her fall from the ladder. She gulped in air and stared down between the rungs. The two Infected below had heard the noise and looked up, hands reaching for her. They tried to jump and clamber up a vertical wooden boundary fence, but their maimed hands could not get any purchase.

"Selena, look at me, not them."

A sweet young voice like an angel cut through the lightheadedness, and she looked up to see Hannah on the far roof smiling at her. The schoolgirl beckoned her over. Selena never had kids, or even wanted them, but if she had she hoped they would have been like Hannah. Gaining strength from the girl on the roof she pulled and scraped her knees bloody crossing the gap. If she could get through this, she would swear as an atheist to any gods listening to keep the girl safe from harm.

Then she was in Hannah's arms. The girl pulled her onto her shaky feet. Selena hugged her tight, partly out of respect and partly knowing that she might fall over otherwise.

"See, piss-easy," Hannah said.

Selena was out of breath and could only laugh in relief as a response.

"Right, Ann next," Tony bellowed.

"What about Ayesha?" Charlie interjected, protective of her step-daughter.

"We ain't got time to draw lots, this ain't a Lesbian Labour Party Conference you know." Tony pointed his large stubby index finger at her.

"Fuck me, let the fat bitch go first, she'll probably fall off anyway," Ayesha said, joining the argument.

"Thanks for that confidence booster, ya skinny whore." Ann entered the fray.

"People, please, somebody go?" Piers tried hard not to shout, trying to calm the situation.

Just then, Brita and Ellie burst through the door and sent the bed frame by the stairwell door down to block it off for a while.

"They are coming," Brita puffed.

Seeing the arguments and confusion, Matt took his chance and climbed on and out of the window before anyone could stop him. He closed his ears to the braying behind him and was across the ladder in record time. He rolled off the end and looked up to see Hannah and Selena frowning down at him.

"You are a woman now then?" Hannah asked him, with a sneer to her voice and lip.

"They were taking too long," he sulkily replied and went off to explore the rear of the roof.

"Ann, come on, you're next," Piers shouted, but the din had been stopped by Brita's chilling announcement. Tony escorted her over to the ladder and helped her up on unsteady wrists onto the ladder.

"Do me proud, show those bitches what you are made of luv," Tony said and then smacked her behind like a horse to get her going. The embarrassment of the group seeing her husband treat her that way, forced her through the window. The padding on her knees and her strong hands served her well. She stuck out her tongue and moved across the ladder at a slow, but steady pace. Her eyes fixed on the roof opposite. When she reached the safety of the other side, she just rolled off onto her back and lay panting with nervous exhaustion. She felt pride in getting across without any major traumas.

"You okay down there?" Selena appeared above her blotting out the white cloud filled sky.

"One up… for fat bitches," She managed to say through her laboured breaths and the sound of her heart pounding in her ears.

"Ayesha you go next," Piers decided he was going to call the shots from now on. If he had to save anyone it was going to be Ayesha for obvious reasons.

Ayesha hugged Charlie and picked up one holdall and slung her arms through the loops like a backpack. She kissed Piers quickly and then hopped up onto the ladder, and crawled through the window in seconds. Then she stood up, much to

Piers' amazement and began to walk across the rungs of the ladder ending up in a run. An amazed looking Hannah caught her at the other end with her mouth agape in wonder at what she had just seen.

"That was frigging cool," Hannah enthused.

"Surbiton High School's top gymnast and runner three years running. Guys *love* a fit bendy girl," Ayesha said and patted Hannah on the bottom as she trotted past, to shrug off the holdall.

"I'm going to check on Steve," Zuzanna said heading down the mezzanine steps, as she hadn't noticed any firing in the past minute.

Only Piers saw her leave. He looked around the rest of the group, weighing up their usefulness and state of minds. There was only one obvious choice to go next. "Ellie you're up."

CHAPTER ELEVEN

ESCAPE?

Brita hurried Ellie over to the ladder. When they reached Piers, she turned to face her girlfriend. "I'm scared, Brita."

"I know, but use that to hurry across, right. Not hold you back."

"You'll come across soon too." Ellie was crying again.

Brita kissed her hard, so their lips and teeth clashed together. It was an urgent show of love and a way to shut Ellie up and get her moving. "Nothing will stop us being together, now get your ass out that window, okay."

"Love you."

"I love you too, but hurry please," Brita said, feeling herself flush with embarrassment on saying aloud what she felt in her heart.

"Okay, I'm going." And she did. Brita watched her proudly, she got off to a nervous, tentative start, but then got into a rhythm and was soon across. Brita smiled at the noises she made traversing the gap and the colourful language she used.

"Brita you can go next if you like." Piers had heard the words of love they had exchanged and didn't want to keep Brita from Ellie any longer than possible.

"Charlie, you're next," Brita called out ignoring him.

"You're a brave lady." Piers said to her.

"I have a gun, don't make me shoot you to shut you up," Brita gave him a deadpan look and then winked at the last second. Charlie had only just reached the ladder when there came a female scream from below.

"Hurry," Brita urged and went to the top of the balcony to investigate.

Charlie scrambled across at breakneck speed with her eyes closed. She nearly fell through the ladder twice and pitched forward and bruised her chest area at one stage. Ayesha dragged her off into a tight bear hug at the end of her short but scary trip, which did her hurting chest no good at all.

"Tony you're up," Piers shouted.

"Really?" Tony had expected to be the last man out. "What about the rugmuncher?" he pointed at Brita.

"Girls with guns go last you sexist fuck," she bit back. "And don't break the ladder on the way over."

Tony muttered under his breath, but not too loudly as he really didn't want to be trapped in the hotel with a hundred skinless maniacs after his slow arse. The trip over was slow and painful on his knees, and the ladder groaned under his weight, as it tested the makers stress limits to the maximum.

"Can you see anything?" Piers called over to Brita as he nervously watched Tony's snail-like progress across the ladder.

"Nothing." The way the rear staircase was set out, you could not see anything until someone or something came through the fire door on the mezzanine floor below.

"Fucking hurry," Piers called out the window.

"Fuck off," Tony shouted back, nearly slipping off the ladder.

Ann gave a squeak of anguish, her hands covering her face, from her vantage point on the roof opposite.

"I'm going down there." Brita moved round to the first step.

A strong hand grabbed her arm and pulled her back. "We can't wait for them. We've got to go, both of us, one after the other. There is no more time left." To prove his point, someone crashed against the third floor barricaded restaurant door.

"Steve, Zuzanna we have to leave," Brita shouted down the stairwell. Piers pulled her again, but she held her ground. No reply came, so she let herself be led over to the ladder.

"You go first, and I'll follow," Piers said racing round to step up on the furthest chair, beside the ladder. He picked up Ann's backpack and put it on.

"No, you first," Brita insisted slinging the rifle strap over her back.

The door opposite screeched in another couple of inches, and two bloody red hands poked through.

"Bloody hell." An exasperated Piers pulled himself onto the ladder and made his way through the window at the speed of someone for whom ladders were part of his daily life. He was glad that Tony had finally made it across to the other side. Brita took one look back, but no one was coming up from the mezzanine floor below. She pulled herself onto the ladder and shimmied through the window.

Something suddenly dragged her back.

Brita panicked for a moment until she saw it was the muzzle of the automatic rifle snagging on the window frame. She ducked down, let out a long breath of relief and hurried on after Piers, who was already across. She remembered her army training of looking up and ahead not down and was soon over, to be smothered with kisses and admonishments from Ellie for not coming across sooner.

"What about the others?" Ayesha asked moving towards the ladder.

"I don't think they are coming," Brita said from Ellie's arms.

"Then we should toss the end of the ladder down to stop those buggers following us." Tony moved over to pick up the ladder and do just that.

"We should give them time," Charlie said rushing over to stop the bent over Tony.

He straightened up, just using his immense frame to cause her to backpedal a little.

"Look!" Ann screamed and pointed across the gap.

A scared and bloodied Zuzanna was forcing her way out of the hotel window, screaming through gritted teeth.

"Come on you can make it," Piers called across to her.

Zuzanna grabbed every rung with intense effort most of her body out of the window. They could see the cuts and bites to her arms and torn clothing. Charlie bent low and reached out her hands across the gap, in a gesture of solidarity, the Polish receptionist was over six feet away. Zuzanna screamed, her mouth wide open in shock, her grip and strength going out of her frame, and she was abruptly pulled a foot back through the broken window. Her face smashed down onto the ladder breaking free a tooth before she was dragged back through the hotel window, screaming. The last thing they saw was her out-stretched hand reaching for them and then she was gone. The screaming lasted five seconds and then came to a gurgling stop.

An infected person appeared at the window, its blood cov-ered exposed teeth biting at the air between them. It began to crawl after them, like some primal creature from humankind's worse nightmare. Tony and Piers sprang into action as others followed it out. They lifted up the ladder with ease and tipped it sideways over the edge of the two-storey building. The Infected fell down and splashed into the flood waters below and on top of some of their own kind.

"Shit," Ann said running her fingers through her hair.

Ellie was crying again.

"How the hell do we get off this roof?" Tony shouted angrily.

"I can't find a trapdoor anywhere," Matt replied, unhelpfully.

"That's just bloody great innit. We go from being trapped in there to trapped on here," he continued to shout and flap his arms about like he might take off and fly to safety.

"Well at least we are still alive, unlike Zuzanna," Brita said, giving Tony her coldest stare.

"What are we going to do?" Ann cried out loudly, stepping in-between Brita and her raging husband, so as to distract them from their continued unhelpful war.

"I've got an idea," Hannah said in a quiet voice.

Selena looked across from where she sat on the roof shiv-ering even with her thickest woolly clothes and coat on and smiled at her child prodigy.

"What you got, sweetie?" Charlie asked moving over to the edge at the front of the building where the schoolgirl knelt.

Ayesha and Piers quickly joined her. The sceptics held their ground while Tony and Brita glared over Ann's head at each other.

"Look, there is a ledge under these windows, we can step on those, then smash one of the windows and get inside. We might find a rear exit away from the Infected." Hannah pointed down, and the others leant over to look.

"Sounds like a good idea to me," Piers said pulling his axe from the back of his braces. "Step back then."

"Good girl," Matt said, giving her the thumbs up from across the roof, which kind of spoilt her moment. Would she always be the young pregnant schoolgirl everyone had to protect and not an integral part of the group? Hannah shook her head and stepped back, as Piers leant over the side holding his axe in both hands. He was perfectly balanced, but Ayesha knelt and held his legs anyway. Closing his eyes, he swung hard with the back of his axe and smashed the middle second-floor window in. With a thankful look at Ayesha, he jumped down onto the ledge and cleaned the edges of the window one-handed with the axe.

"Right, I'll scout the place out, hold up here." He was through the window before Ayesha could even get the words *good luck* formed on her lips. Hannah moved up and rubbed her back and was rewarded with a thankful smile from the other teenager.

The Infected were glaring at them from below and the hotel window they had escaped from, unnerving the grouped stranded for the time being on the damp flat roof.

"You think we should go after him?" Ayesha said to Hannah, not feeling that brave, but feeling she needed Piers more than any other man in her life.

"No need," Hannah pointed down.

"Hello." Piers poked his head out of the window below them. "The place is empty and secure, so start sending people down."

The ledge was quite wide with an ornamental wooden awning angling down under it, and a safe drop down from the flat roof above. Ayesha went first, making a little of a meal of it, just to cling to Pier's arms and chest as he helped her inside. Hannah had to smile at herself despite the situation, Ayesha was the type of girl that always got her man. One by one they transferred from the roof to inside the upper office of the building. Piers had to bring Selena down clinging to his back for dear life, but they all made it into the two-storey office building without any drama.

"What do we do now?" Ann asked loitering with Tony by the open stairs to more office space below.

"See if there is a way out the back and away from this dead town," Piers said striding for the stairs. No one could disagree with his appraisal of the situation, so grabbed what stuff they had and followed him downstairs. The ground floor of the office computer company was under two feet of water. Papers, pencils, and business cards floated in the murky waters, but the front door was locked and keeping the Infected out at least. Piers led them to a staff restroom kitchenette area at the rear of the building. There was a rear door and a large window over a metal sink. They all splashed inside peering through the window into a fenced off rear car park for the surrounding businesses. There were only one or two Infected lurking about around the half-submerged cars.

"What do we do now?" Ann asked, having to go on the tips of her toes to peer out the window.

"I say we run for it. Make for the railway tracks again and head south out of here," Selena said.

"Can't see you pegging it anywhere luv, but I agree," Tony gave her an almost respectful nod.

"Then we move fast. Brita, you take the lead, and I'll bring up the rear. Matt and Charlie, it's your job to help Selena along, carry her if you have too. We are all going for this and getting out of it alive, okay," Piers said, moving to the back door. He tried the handle and then laughed.

"What's wrong honey?" Ayesha asked, edging closer, her movement making a bow wave through the flood waters.

"It's locked," Piers smiled back at everyone, a little relief on his tense young face. He hefted his axe. "We will soon sort that."

"Get ready," Brita said to Ellie pulling her by the arm closer to her.

Piers smashed the door open, but it stuck with the weight of the water behind it. He had to shoulder barge it fully open so everyone could get through. An Infected person was making a bee-line for him as he emerged from the back door of the office. He swung his axe, remembering what they had done to poor Zuzanna only moments ago. His axe blade caught the poor creature in the neck severing its skinless head from its shoulders. Both body parts splashed under the water five feet away from each other.

"Come on." He waved them on from the safety of the office building.

Brita came first dragging Ellie after her. They splashed across the car park as another Infected appeared from behind a half-submerged blue Peugeot. Brita stopped, steadied herself as it ran towards her and Ellie, wearing the remains of a Policewoman's uniform. Brita shot it in the chest, sending it down under the flood waters for good. Across the private parking area, there was an open door to some type of restaurant kitchens. She and Ellie splashed through the flood waters, hoping it would lead through to the next road and bring them closer to the railway tracks.

Behind them, Piers was waving everyone through after them. Only when the last of the group was gone did he follow after watching their backs. Luckily the main group of Infected that had invaded the hotel hadn't found out where they had gone yet. He followed after Tony and Ann, slowing to match their speed.

Ahead, Ellie tripped and fell with a splash. Brita dragged her spluttering and retching from the water and through the open door into the kitchen of a kebab house. She had to let her girlfriend go to scope out the small kitchen. Two men in dirty white t-shirts and aprons were floating face down near a slightly open walk-in fridge. Brita pressed on hoping Ellie would stop coughing and retching soon. Brita hurried through an opening, a toilet was to her left and some steep stairs to her right. Ahead led through to a counter with other cooking appliances with rotting floating food everywhere. Brita sped around the counter to see that the tables and chairs ahead were empty. The entrance to the kebab shop was predominantly glass.

"You okay?" She quickly asked Ellie.

Ellie, who was still coughing and crying, gave her a weak thumbs up. Brita hurried over to peer through the glass fronted door of the kebab shop onto the road ahead. There seemed nothing moving outside, either people or Infected. She unlocked the latches of the shop door. Hannah and Ayesha soon joined them, as she unlocked the door and moved outside into the next empty street.

Ahead of them was a brown brick building almost Japanese in design. The main part of the four-story building was set back with the side coming out closer to the road. There was a square submerged courtyard edged with green trees and well tended raised brick planting beds. Yet, inside the square, lined with metal poles to prevent people parking there, floated at least thirty dead uninfected human bodies of all ages, sexes, and races.

Behind Brita, Ellie did throw up this time.

CHAPTER TWELVE

FREEDOM, BUT AT WHAT COST?

They all hurried through the kebab shop until only Piers was left at the rear. All of the escaping group stopped liked Brita and Ellie before them, paralysed by the sight of so many corpses.

Piers made sure that no Infected were after him and turned to close the door to the park area behind him. He was so busy bolting the door and bending over to turn the key in the lock that he did not see the door to the walk-in fridge open. Nor the figure fly out at him until it was too late.

Tony and Ann were last out of the shop and stopped beside Matt and Charlie, who were helping Selena. Ayesha was carrying a bag of supplies and Matt had Selena's pack on.

"What a senseless waste of human life," Selena said solemnly.

"We need to keep moving, we can't help them, only ourselves," Brita stated and moved off round to the right of the building where a side road led hopefully back to where the railways tracks were. They knew that the roads were pretty impassable in many areas, and the return to the tracks was a place they felt a little safer and was mostly above flood levels.

Ellie wiped her mouth on her damp sleeve and wished for a polo mint right now. The others turned away from the grisly sight and peeled away after the former Danish soldier.

"Hey, where's Piers?" Ayesha looked back towards the shop. Her friend with benefits was nowhere to be seen.

"Go get him, I'll wait here for you," Hannah urged her.

Ayesha looked at Charlie and the rest of the group making for the side road and then splashed back through the flood waters and into the kebab shop again. "Piers? What's keeping you, babe?" She yelled at the edge of the food counter. She waded through the bobbing onions and fatty deposits floating on the surface with a wrinkled up nose. "Piers?"

She moved through the small corridor and saw the bodies of the kitchen staff floating in the water. Yet she swore there had only been two when she came through a minute or so ago.

"Piers hon-ey." Her voice cracked halfway through the second word. The third body floating face down near the closed back door had a knife sticking up from his back and blood diluting the water around it. Ayesha took a shaky step inside the kitchen as air bubbled up from around the face of the fresh kill and it half turned over to reveal Piers' dead un-focused eyes and wide open mouth. Ayesha screamed, and turned and ran from the kitchen. She screamed as the air was punched out of her, as a woman leapt down from the stairs above knocking her through into the counter area. Ayesha bounced off the side of the open doorway and landed down on her side, scrambling to hold on to the side of a counter to keep her head above water. The wild looking made woman had fallen into the hallway toilet door and stunned herself, but not for long. She rounded the corner, no signs of obvious infection on her skin, her eyes wide and unblinking, her mouth open and screaming at Ayesha.

Ayesha scrambled back, and her hand grabbed a can of cream soda. The woman leapt on her, grabbing and scratching at Ayesha's throat. All Ayesha could do was bring the can down onto the woman's nose five times quickly in a row, breaking it and sending blood everywhere.

Hannah walked into the kebab shop to find a manic looking woman with wild bedraggled hair and a bloodied nose trying to force Ayesha's head under water. Hannah looked around, but the rest of the group were far away rounding the corner of the brown building. She dropped the bag she had on a table, picked up a wooden chair and smashed it hard over the back of the woman's head. Unlike a thousand films she had seen, the chair did not splinter into many pieces, but it did knock the woman out cold. Ayesha pushed the crazy woman off her and let her slip under the water.

Hannah helped Ayesha up and then went to pull the woman up and stop her from drowning.

"Leave her, she killed my Piers," Ayesha said in a cold tone.

"Where?"

"In the kitchen." Ayesha pointed but did not move. Hannah hurried past the woman's body which had floated up to the surface and took a look for herself. She came back thirty seconds later in tears carrying Pier's fireman's axe. Ayesha was standing where she had left her, but her right foot was holding the crazy woman underwater, just to make sure she was dead.

"I'm so sorry, Ayesha, I know you liked him," Hannah said, edging around the counter to avoid touching the submerged dead woman.

"I loved him," Ayesha stated, looking at her blankly. "I hardly fucking knew him and I loved him, and now he's dead like my mum."

Hannah got to the edge of the counter, but was blocked off by Ayesha and the woman's corpse. "Sorry," Hannah said again, knowing the words were no help to Ayesha, her or anyone else at the moment.

"I didn't even get to tell him or say goodbye."

"We need to catch up with the others and Charlie." Hannah hoped the mention of her other mum would get her moving.

"Give me the axe."

Hannah stared from the vague shape of the woman Ayesha held underwater up to the teenager's face. She didn't want to give it over, not knowing what might happen next, but it belonged to Piers, so Ayesha should have claim to it. Hannah timidly handed the axe to Ayesha's outstretched hand. Ayesha with no tears in her eyes took it and stepped off the woman's corpse. It floated up to the brown surface but did not move.

"Come on," Ayesha said as she turned and waded out of the kebab shop. Hannah took one look at the opening to the kitchen where Piers floated dead and followed after Ayesha. Hannah had like Piers, even fancied him a bit. It felt wrong to just leave him behind in the greasy back of a kebab shop. In this new flooded world of danger and disease, there was no way to bury or burn the dead anyway. She splashed after Ayesha; she would need her friendship now more than ever.

"Hang on where are the others?" Ann was puffed out and blowing. She had stopped to look back down the way they had come to the corner of the brown building.

"Brita," Charlie called to stop the Danish woman hurrying on through the ankle-deep flood waters.

"What!" Brita replied in a loud dismissive voice.

"My Ayesha, Hannah, and Piers aren't behind us," Charlie said in a worried voice. She and Matt were helping the under-the-weather Selena along.

"They will catch up." Brita frowned looking from the corner then down to a lush green embankment beyond. She could see part of the metal frame of a set of signals through a line of trees, their escape to the railways tracks was nearly complete. She hesitated, not wanting to go back for stragglers. Ellie came first.

"We've got to go back for them," Selena pleaded.

"Or are you scared, Abba chick," Tony taunted.

"I'm Danish, you fucking moron," Brita spat as she unslung her automatic rifle. "Keep them moving," she said to Ellie and ran to the rear of the group.

"Hurry back," Ellie croaked, her voice still a bit raw from vomiting up flood water.

Brita ran splashing through the water, back the way they had come down the side road. She nearly got to the corner when two running figures appeared, she raised the rifle in self-defence, but lowered it quickly when she saw it was Ayesha and Hannah.

"Glad you could make it," Brita said, looking past the two teen girls as they slowed to a walk. "Where's Piers?"

"He ain't coming," Ayesha said in a flat voice as she walked past holding his fireman's axe.

Brita looked at Hannah, her lips pressed together in concern.

"Some mad woman stabbed him, he's dead," Hannah managed to get out before the tears came. She hurried after the fast striding Ayesha, leaving Brita rooted to the spot.

"Fuck it." Brita turned and stomped after them. He had been the only man in the group that she had any respect for.

Ellie and Tony were at the end of the road that led to the car park that led up an overgrown embankment. Tony was kicking down a boundary fence covered with bushes and green leaves. A gentle rutted path made by foxes led up through the undergrowth to the railway tracks above.

"There you are, I was worried about you, Ash," Charlie said with a relieved laugh, as Ayesha passed her, Selena, and Matt by to head for the fence. Tony was having trouble with a tough twisted branch that was keeping the fence upright, even though he kept on kicking at it.

Ayesha walked up, swung the axe overhead and brought it down on the branch severing it in one go. Tony's right foot was only a couple of inches away from the axe blade as the fence collapsed into the ferns and grass. Ayesha, with only a slight grunt pulled up the axe and trudged silently up the embankment first.

"Mind me foot, you silly moo," Tony bellowed after her.

Ayesha just ignored him and walked up onto the tracks.

"What's wrong darling?" Charlie called after her.

"Yeah what's her problem?" Tony said to Charlie.

"Piers is dead," Hannah managed to get out before the weight of all the grief buckled her strong young shoulders.

"Aw, fuck," Tony stated, which was as near as he got to compassion.

"How?" Ann waded over to comfort Hannah, but she could not force a reply out.

"Some mad woman killed him apparently," Brita said, bringing up the rear. "We need to keep moving."

"I've got to go to her," Charlie apologised to Selena as she left her side and ran to the embankment.

"Go," Selena urged.

Charlie hurried up the embankment slipping twice on the greasy leaves and mud. She found Ayesha standing in the middle of eight railway tracks in and out of the nearby station. She had Piers's axe in her hands and was just staring down the tracks into the distance.

"You okay, Ash?" Charlie asked moving around to the side of her. She wanted to get into her line of vision, so as not to startle her.

"Where do you think we should head next?" Ayesha said in a cold voice like the colourful happy-go-lucky girl had been washed out.

"I guess we will all decide it together," Charlie stumbled over her words. She sniffed and wiped the tears from the tip of her nose as she felt for Ayesha.

"I was shit at geography at school. As long as I know where the shops and clubs are, I'm okay. I should have studied more. Being good at tanning people ain't no fucking use is it." Ayesha continued to stare down the tracks as Charlie edged closer.

"But you cut hair too, people will always need that hun." Charlie moved next to Ayesha and put her arm around her.

"Yeah, suppose," Ayesha replied.

They didn't speak again. The rest of the group moving in mournful silence soon joined them. They walked together as a loose group. Mourning for Piers, but also relived to be out of the dirty flood waters again.

CHAPTER THIRTEEN

WALKING THROUGH A SUNKEN DREAM

They walked on down the tracks until they split into two different routes, which forced the party from its silence.

"Anyone know which way goes where?" Ann asked, looking from one direction to the next.

"Don't ask me," Brita shrugged.

"That way heads towards Farnborough and the other way down to Guildford," Matt spoke up.

"How did you know that?" Selena asked him.

"Trainspotter?" Tony suggested.

"Geography teacher." Matt frowned at the large man's back. Hannah managed to smile at him, which lifted his spirits. In the desperate escape from Woking, he had nearly forgotten she was carrying his child.

"So do we head for Farnborough like the soldiers suggested and hope they haven't been overrun, or Guildford, and hope that it hasn't fallen? And if they have, where do we head then, we need a backup plan," Selena said.

"We need a bleedin' first plan, first," Tony grunted.

"Maybe we should head to the coast, get a ferry to the Isle of Wight or France?" Charlie suggested.

"I doubt if we could get anywhere with the south of England quarantined. Lots of Naval bases down on the coast, bet they are well guarded." Matt warned of the possible dangers.

"Anything on your mobile phone?" Ellie asked him.

"Not a thing; no bars, no signal, no internet, no way to know if we are walking into danger whichever way we choose." Matt stared at his useless mobile phone.

"What route takes us closer to the coast?" Brita asked, wondering if she and Ellie could find a small boat and sail round to Denmark and safety.

"Much of a muchness," Matt said, bringing a shrug of lost-in-translation from Brita. "We want to head to Portsmouth for the naval bases and ports like Southampton. We need to head south-west and both kind of head that way. Guildford is the shortest route to the actual coast, though."

"Then I guess we vote Farnborough or Guildford?" Hannah said pointing to each route in turn.

"I vote Farnborough and hope the armed forces are still there, evacuating people," Tony said staring at Ann.

"Farnborough," she said on automatic.

"Guildford," Brita said.

"Guildford," Ellie said, holding onto her lover's arm.

"Farnborough," Charlie said.

"Farnborough," Hannah said.

"Farnborough, fingers crossed," Matt said, giving his choice. He would not leave his unborn child for a second time.

"Guildford, not that it matters now," Selena said, knowing the vote was already lost.

"Ayesha what about you?" Hannah asked her.

"Wherever, don't matter does it," she said heading towards Farnborough. "We are all going to die whichever way we go."

Charlie hurried after her, but could not get any serious replies out of her for the rest of the day.

"Farnborough it is then," Brita muttered as she slung her rifle and taking Ellie's hand, headed after Ayesha and Charlie.

"Don't matter where we go as long as we are together," Ellie whispered in her ear and then kissed her cheek. Brita smiled at her, she was right of course, and at least the tracks were above the flood waters. They all trudged on again, with wet shoes, socks, feet and ankles.

Once the decision which tracks they were taking was over, silence descended over the group again. Woking had been an eye opener for all of them. They headed towards Farnborough more out of hope than expectations of getting rescued. It was cold, with a stiff north-easterly breeze, but at least it was dry underfoot and not raining. They were safe for the time being, with trees and bushes masking either side of them again. Back to their own little bubble world, while the rest of Britain carried on around them. It took them over an hour to walk slowly along to the next station. Either side of the tracks was flooded, but the station was on a slight rise. A vast cemetery was on the left-hand side, with only the tops of gravestones and tombs showing. The waters shimmered reflecting the dull daylight as it covered the final resting places of so many dead.

They wanted to rest and eat so badly, but it was not to be. Brita and Ellie scouted into the station buildings, only to witness three Infected chasing and capturing a young teenage girl, before biting her to death. They saw this through a dirty window, glad that the station doors were locked up tight. They turned and hurried back to the group, who mournfully decided the only action was to move on quickly.

It was a bitter blow to Ann the most; she was starving, thirsty and dead on her feet as it was. She trudged on, her legs aching and her shoes rubbing making blisters. She wasn't even sure if life was worth all this effort anymore. Her family was gone if it weren't for Tony she'd just sit down on the tracks and wait to die. Tony would pull her up by the hair if she tried to give up, he still needed her in his way. Yet his ways were often dark and brutal.

The group hurried from the station until the fear spent adrenaline left them feeling cold. They stopped to eat and rest as best they could in their little cliques. The conversations were muted at best, and they knew they had to find somewhere safe to shelter before dark. With trips to the left for the women and right for the men to do what comes naturally, they set off again. The pace was up awhile but then sagged to a slow trudge. Even Brita and some of the younger members of the group were suffering from physical and mental fatigue. The houses and cemetery were soon replaced by a wall of trees and near impenetrable hedges and thickets. Their journey became an endless monotony of tracks leading off into the distance and hedging greenery, nothing else but that and the grey cloudy sky.

The route seemed to keep them away from civilisation, as it was. Which kept them in the dark on how vast the flooding was around them and how far the infection had spread? The only blessing was they were away from people, away from the Infected, which meant the chances of them coming down with it were less than most people.

The dry tracks soon ended as a canal on one side, and a huge pond on the other had merged to cover a dip in the tracks. Once again they had to wade through, up to their knees at certain points. This did not help to improve anyone's mood. It took them fifteen minutes to pass through the stagnant water, and everyone was feeling heavy of heart, mind, and limbs when they reached the other side.

"We need to find somewhere to rest, my Ann is nearly dead on her feet here," Tony called from way back where he and his wife were lagging behind.

"He's right," Selena said, hating to agree with the chauvinistic man. She was near to collapse. "We need to find shelter sooner, rather than later."

Brita nodded from the front, she had led the way since leaving Woking. She and Ellie looked around, they could see nothing but trees, fields, and flooded areas. "As soon as we spot somewhere habitable and safe we will stop, for sure."

"I'm knackered," Matt said sitting down on one rail.

"I can't go any further, sorry," Selena apologised.

Brita looked around the group. They were all tired and demoralised about losing Piers. Ayesha, usually so chatty hadn't spoken in an hour. They weren't going anywhere without a morale boost.

"Look Ellie and I will scout ahead while everyone rests up. We will find somewhere safe ahead to spend the night," Brita said to everyone.

"And then come back and get you all," Ellie added for her. Yet that had not been in Brita's thinking at all. Apart from three of the women, she didn't care if she never saw any of the others again. She could quite easily leave them all here to fend for themselves if she had Ellie by her side. Yet, Ellie would never go for that, she had a soft heart, and that's why she loved her.

"I'll come too," Ayesha said.

"Don't you want to rest, hun?" Charlie approached her and tried to hug her from behind.

Ayesha flinched away from her touch. "I'm not tired, let's go." She stomped off along the track, and Brita turned and followed her.

"We'll take good care of her." Ellie comforted Charlie with a wave. "We will be back before you know it."

Not if I had my way, Brita thought in Danish.

The trio walked on at a brisk pace now they had left the others behind. After fifteen minutes, they had only spotted a submerged barn in the middle of a field. They were about to stop and turn back when Ayesha bent down on her haunches and peered through a thinner line of trees and bushes.

"What can you see?" Brita stopped and headed back to her, with Ellie in her wake.

"I think I can see a swimming pool?" Ayesha said, in a slightly bemused voice.

Ellie looked up and pointed. "Look."

Brita and Ayesha craned their heads up to see electricity poles and lines crossing the tracks above their heads and disappearing into the tree line they were looking through.

"Can't be a coincidence," Ellie said, "and I think I can see the edge of a big house down there."

"Let's go check it out," Ayesha said gripping the axe tight in her hands. She entered the tree line and up a rise that had been cut back in the last year compared to the surrounding high foliage. At the top of the rise, she could see the edges of a flood-free well-tended lawn, a large open-air swimming pool, tennis courts and a large mansion that could easily sell for five million pounds in this neck-of-the-woods. Ayesha hoped to hell that it was empty, and the owners were sunning themselves somewhere on a sandy foreign beach. The large home and huge one-storey garage were built on a small hill, with a long private drive that wound through the trees and out of sight.

"I wonder if there is any room at the inn?" Ellie wondered aloud.

"I hope that no one is in, and we can have the run of the place," Ayesha stated.

"Even if there are people there, I'm sure they would help us," Ellie said hopefully.

Brita said nothing. The rich often think they have a lot more to protect than more generous poor people, in her opinion. Even if there was someone there, she had the rifle to persuade them to let them stay the night. "Let us go and see if anyone is at home."

The three women made their way down the other side of the rise and into the gardens of the mansion. There were no boundary fences, as the place only had the railway line and woods behind it. They skirted the large pool onto some Italian flagstones that formed a path around the building. There were large french windows with cream blinds pulled behind them.

"Let's head round to the front door," Ellie suggested, knowing Brita and Ayesha might just smash their way in otherwise. She still held firm to her beliefs of law and order, even under these difficult times.

The other two followed her around the impressive building, which looked like it had bedrooms in the double figure mark. The flagstones led through a rose bush covered arch and then through a box hedge path around to the raised pillared front double pale blue doors.

Ellie stepped up and pulled at a black iron chime to the right of the doors and waited. Ellie looked back to see Brita holding the automatic rifle ready at the door. "Gun," she chided.

Brita frowned and lowered the rifle end to the floor, but did not sling it. Ayesha too let the axe head lower, to rest against her left ankle.

"Right, best smiles girls," Ellie ordered as they heard someone approach the front doors.

Hannah brought a bottle of orange flavoured water over to where Charlie was standing and just staring at the bend in the tracks waiting for Ayesha and the others to return. They thought they had heard a gunshot earlier, and this made them all jumpy and concerned.

"Drink?"

"Thanks," Charlie said with the briefest acknowledgement that Hannah was there and took the bottle from her, but just held it tight with both hands.

"I'm sure they will be back soon," Hannah said, but it sounded like a weak platitude even as she said it.

"Mmhmm." Charlie nodded.

Hannah could not think of another helpful word to say, so just stood next to Charlie watching the empty tracks with her. It was another seven minutes before they spotted a single female figure hurrying back towards them. It took a few seconds to realise it was Ellie, and she was jogging towards them. Charlie and Hannah shared a look of concern. Everyone stood up and waited for Ellie to arrive and wondered with trepidation why she was alone and what sort of tale she had to tell.

CHAPTER FOURTEEN

THE BIG HOUSE

"Where's my Ayesha, is she alright?" Charlie called, running a few feet up the tracks to meet the exhausted looking Ellie.

Ellie raised her finger as she caught her breath. "We...we found...a big house."

"And Ayesha, is she and Brita okay?" Charlie asked putting her cold, pale hands on Ellie's face.

"Both fine," Ellie nodded and then pointed at the water Charlie was carrying. "May I?"

"Oh, course darling," Charlie said unscrewing the top and handing the bottle over to Ellie. She drank her fill and then handed it back to Charlie who took a swig.

"So we have someplace to stay tonight then?" Ann asked joining them.

"Yes...it's some place alright. Wait until you see it, bedrooms for all of us, grab your stuff come on, let's be having you."

And they all followed after Ellie with renewed vigour in their strides.

Ellie led them down the slope and around the huge house, just as Ayesha threw a bucket of water over a large puddle of blood on the raised entrance step. The pink liquid ran down the steps to greet the rest of the group. Brita appeared behind her and did the same with a washing up bowl. The area smelt of bleach.

"Ash you are alright," Charlie half-wailed with delight as she rushed up the wet steps to hug the air out of her adopted daughter, causing her to drop the bucket. "Are you okay darling?"

"I'm fine," Ayesha said trying to wriggle from Charlie's tight embrace. "Look, come inside, I'll show you around." Ayesha offered just to get Charlie to let her go and breathe properly.

The others hurried up the steps after Ayesha and Charlie. Brita stepped to the side to let them through. Ellie kissed her cheek as she went past, causing Brita to blush a little.

"Trouble?" Selena asked looking down at the running watered-down blood river flowing down one edge of the steps.

"Nothing Ayesha and me could not handle."

Selena was worried about the cold look in Brita's eyes and wondered what had gone on here at the front step of this massive mansion. Then she remembered the high horse she had fallen off and closed her mouth. She was still weak and tired and just wanted a soft bed to collapse on or even the nearest settee.

Brita tapped the stock of the rifle slung over her back as the last of the group went inside. She scanned the woods opposite for a few seconds and then went in and locked the big heavy doors behind her. She wandered past the group and ignored their questions. She wanted to do another circuit of the large house and check every room again. She didn't want anything to surprise them overnight. Not like the front door. That had nearly ended in disaster. She pushed the images of blood and death from her mind or at least to the far reaches of her Id where the dark hobgoblin nightmares held reign. They would have questions first, and then she and Ellie would check the house out again and find a plush double bedroom for the night.

Matt helped Selena over to a sofa in a vast living room with the whitest plumpest shag pile he'd ever seen. He put her pack next to her feet as she lay down and almost instantly fell asleep. He hurried after the group who were making a beeline for the cavernous white and black marble kitchen. The owners sure had a thing for black and white colour schemes and wondered if the magnolia hallway was as far onto the colour wheel as their designers went.

"So what happened at the step and all that blood?" Charlie

moved closer to Ayesha touching the back of her hair in a caring way.

"Nothing," Ayesha flinched away from her and covered it up by walking over to a wine rack and pulling a bottle of red out. "Who fancies a drink? Cos I sure do."

"Then why won't you tell me?" Charlie strode over, not letting it go.

"Cos there is nothing much to tell, we had a situation and dealt with it. Now be useful Charlie and find me a corkscrew."

"You can tell me then?" Charlie homed in on Brita and Ellie her finger pointing at Brita.

"The previous owners attacked us so we retaliated with force. That is all." Brita simply replied.

"And they were infected, right?"

Brita nodded. "We put on rubber gloves and dragged them to the garage and then washed our hands and disinfected the front porch."

"What's the big deal, we have a place to stay for the night and food and booze," Tony said, checking a low cooler for beer.

"Let's just find a room and then get out of our wet clothes for a while, then meet back here in an hour or so to eat. How does that sound?" Hannah said, tired of bickering and company for a while.

"Sounds good to me," Matt said.

Hannah did not make eye contact with him. She headed off upstairs with most of the group looking for a bedroom for the night she would sleep in alone. She found a lovely little attic room, with a tiny en-suite and washed her aching feet and ankles in the bath before lying on the bed to rest. She found sleep easy to come by.

Brita and Ayesha did one last sweep of the house to make sure it was secure while Ellie found a bedroom with a huge four-poster bed. Ellie was smiling, opening wardrobe doors full of expensive women's clothing. In a drawer, she found a knee length silk negligee and threw off her damp clothes and quickly pulled it on over her shivering body. She washed her face, hands and feet in the en-suite bathroom and dabbed on some perfume. She hurried off and jumped into the plush bed to warm up and wait for Brita, she would give her the night of her life. Her smile was wide as she waited, thinking of the kisses she would plant all over her lover's body.

Then an image of the front door opening flashed into her mind like a lightning bolt. Her smile collapsed like she was having a stroke, her shoulder slumped, and her eyes became fixed on a picture of a fox hunt on the opposite wall. She saw the fear in the painted fox's eyes as it fled the hounds and red-coated men on horseback. She saw the door of this big mansion open again and again, playing the moment over and over. Her mind could not get past the door opening and the couple inside coming out to greet them. She saw it all, again and again, making her put her hands in her hair and drag her nails through her scalp until she drew blood. Her lips trembled. She could almost hear the horn sounding in the hunt picture on the wall. Then she recalled shouting, anger, a raised weapon and then blood and thunder. Then she was running back to the group to get them, the house was secure. Ellie looked down at her hands and saw the blood and hair under her nails.

"Now that won't do for my Brita," she said, smiling once more. She hopped out of bed and into the bathroom to scrub them clean under the cold tap. Her hands were pink and raw when Brita finally found her in the bedroom. Ellie smothered her with kisses as soon as she entered the bedroom and began tearing at Brita's clothes.

Brita was surprised at first, but Ellie's kisses and the way the silk clung to her lover's body soon took every thought from her mind. She pulled the silk lingerie over her girlfriend's head, and they staggered in each other's naked embrace to the warmer confines of the bed.

"I'll go find us a room then," Charlie said to Ayesha after five minutes' awkward silence in the large kitchen.

Ayesha nodded from her position sitting up on one of the cold marble counters. She had found a battery powered corkscrew, but no glasses so was swigging the vintage red wine from the bottle.

"You sure you are okay?" Charlie asked, from the doorway.

"No, but I'll live," she said and raised the £50 bottle of wine by the neck in salute.

"It will get better." Charlie's words trailed off to a whisper. She headed up the grand staircase, not believing what she had said either.

Ayesha, alone in the kitchen, stared at the cupboard to her left. Inside was a bin with bloodied paper towels where she had cleaned off the axe she had used during the attack at the front door. She tried not to think of the heavy thunk the axe made as it sunk into flesh and bone of the lady of the house. She swallowed some more wine and forced herself to think of Piers' face. Already it was hard to remember all his handsome features. She just saw his dead eyes in the water staring up and not seeing her. She tried thinking of something else, but all her mind recalled was the woman's shock as the axe sunk deep into her and her collapsing in a pool of blood on the front step.

Ayesha drank again until the images began to blur and fog in her mind. Her stomach rumbled, but she ignored it. Instead, she put down the empty bottle, hopped off the counter and went to fetch another one. She chose white this time, ignoring her mum's sage-like voice in her head about mixing her drinks. She continued drinking until her late mother's voice, the woman's and Piers' corpses disappeared into a drunken fog. Only then did she stagger out of the kitchen. She only made it as far as a sofa in the drawing-room, before collapsing into a fitful drunken stupor.

Ann and Tony found a large bedroom overlooking the rear of the house. They were glad to get their wet clothes off, and she found them some clothes in a hope chest at the end of the bed. They were not modern, but remarkably she found shoes, trousers, and shirts to fit her Tony and some stuff for her as well. Someone older, and twenty years out of style had once lived in this house and had been a giant of a man like her husband. She had to find Tony a belt, the trousers were his regular size, but exercise and lack of food lately had meant he had lost weight.

They ate some snacks on the bed before Tony kissed her tenderly and made for the door.

"Where are you off to you big lug?"

"To find how expensive whisky tastes. Don't worry I'll bring the bottle and two glasses back."

"I normally only like *Jack* and Coke, though."

"Then we will have to slum it with the hoity-toity posh stuff eh," he laughed and left the room.

Ann raised her eyebrows and closed her open mouth.

"Where is my rude hubby and what have you done with him," she said to the closed door. "Not that I'm complaining."

And she started on another bag of prawn cocktail crisps.

Charlie had found a twin bedroom at the far end of the house. It was decorated with kids in mind, but the beds looked very comfy to her. She wandered about the room looking at pictures of strangers in frames. Some riding horses, one with two smiling girls on a jet ski somewhere abroad with an azure sea.

She found some jeans to fit her and socks and trainers in a white wardrobe and put them on. Her toes still felt icy cold, but she had terrible circulation at the best of times. At least her feet and ankles were dry, for the time being. She recalled Pam used to shriek when she put her cold bed feet on hers at night. Pam's body had always been warm and comforting, now she would never feel that love and safety again.

Charlie exhaled and wiped a tear from her right cheek. She wandered out of the bedroom to find a toilet and sob her heart out for a while.

Selena's dream of an ice-cream parlour in Tuscany changed dramatically to a wet night in Surrey and the bump as her car hit the unseen cyclist. She moaned and turned into the settee in her sleep, but did not wake.

Matt sat on a double bed, stripped of his shoes, socks, and trousers. They lay in a dropped heap, half-inside-out where he'd left them. He was thinking of Ellie and Hannah; two women he had had in his life until both relationships had suddenly come to an end. Ellie was lost to him with that *Danish Dyke* about, but Hannah had no one, and she was carrying his child. He was sure that she would take him back when she realised how hard it would be coping alone as she got bigger during the pregnancy.

An image of her in her school uniform with her crisp white shirt tied up over exposed baby bump, had given him a sudden rock hard-on in his boxers. He smiled, yes she would take him back. He just had to play the long game and box clever with her teen hormonal emotions. He reached inside his boxers and grabbed himself tightly, the game wasn't over yet.

Charlie washed her face and went downstairs to check on Selena. She was still asleep. So she went back into the kitchen, but Ayesha was not there. She saw that it would be getting dark outside soon so rummaged through the drawers for a while. She found two torches; a long handled electric gas lighter, two boxes of matches and a box of unused white candles. Taking one of the torches, she went around the downstairs of the house to familiarise herself with it.

In the drawing-room she found Ayesha passed out, drooling and snoring in equal measure. Charlie kissed her head, fearing how it would feel when she woke up. Then a dark thought entered her mind, and she headed quickly to the front doors. There seemed to be no one about downstairs who was awake, so she unbolted and unlocked the front doors and slipped outside. The sun was setting behind the surrounding trees making the intermittent clouds glow pink, orange, and yellow. Looking at the sky, she wondered how there could be so much death and disease under such a lovely sunset.

Charlie turned right and headed along the box-edged path to the end of the house and then crossed a gravel road to the large garage. She couldn't figure out how to open the large car doors, but she spotted a single side entrance. The door was closed, but thankfully unlocked. She turned the handle and pulled the door open. Her hand felt slick, and she looked at her palm to see a smear of blood across her lifeline. She wiped it quickly against the back of her jeans and hurried inside the gloomy garage, turning the torch on.

The light switches on the wall did not work, so she moved the beam of the torch from side-to-side to get her bearings.

There were six cars inside; three hidden under beige covers. The others were a Jag, a Ferrari and a Range Rover. Over to the right near a workbench full of shiny metal tools was another beige cover, but it was hiding something else on the garage floor. A trail of dragged blood led to it.

Charlie stopped. Breathing hard, she tried to keep down the gorge rising in her throat. She leant forward to move, but only the upper half of her body dipped a little forward. Her legs were fixed to the spot, and she just rocked backwards instead. She licked her dry lips and then immediately wiped off the excess moisture with the palm of her free hand. She turned on the spot and then back again.

"This is stupid," she said to the empty garage. It was cold, and she could see her breath in the torchlight, fanning out before her. Then she moved quickly before she lost her bottle, grabbing the cover and retreated while holding it. It slid off to reveal two corpses. Charlie put her free hand to her mouth to stop from crying out and flicked the torchlight away from the two bodies to the workbench. She wished Pam was here, being a nurse she would have seen these sights hundreds of times.

"Come on, come on. You've come this far girl."

Charlie slowly moved the shaking torch beam over the bodies again. One was a woman, probably blonde and pretty in life, in her early forties. Her face was splattered with blood as there was a vicious penetrating wound going halfway through her neck. Charlie wiped her dry lips with her palm and held it there. She inched forwards to look at the man beside her. Probably her husband. He looked older, with a plump well-lived face, he looked at least fifteen years the woman's senior. He had a blackened hole in his left cheek the size of a five pence piece and one side of the back of his head seemed missing.

Charlie pulled the cover down, moved and flicked the torch beam over their bodies.

Neither of them showed any visible sign of infection.

CHAPTER FIFTEEN

FRACTURED

Hannah yawned as she came down the stairs after night had fallen. It was cold in the big house, but better than being outside, she knew that. There was a glow about the place, and she frowned until Matt appeared carrying four candles in one hand and a box of matches in the other.

"Let there be light," he said lighting a candle before sticking it in a silver candlestick on an ornamental Chinese looking table nearby. He handed it to Hannah as she made it to the bottom step.

"Thanks," she smiled at him.

"There is a real fireplace in the big living room, I thought we could get it going. Do you want to give me a hand, it's okay if you don't." Matt lit another candle and placed it in the next candlestick.

Hannah studied his face. She was wary of him, but his face looked sincere enough."Okay."

"Cool," he said and led the way into the living room, where Selena snored gently.

Hannah smiled at his back. She used to tease him about saying *cool* and words like *sick*, just to pretend he was down with the kids. *Down with the kids? He was bloody fucking one of them.* Hannah let a laugh escape.

Matt turned around and smiled at her. That smile, the winning come to bed, or the back of my car smile she had fallen for like she was a stupid Disney Princess. "You okay?"

"Yeah, don't mind me." She waved him on towards the big

open fireplace. "So apart from Selena, have you seen anyone else about?"

"Saw Charlie earlier, but she blanked me. Had a face like absolute thunder. She went upstairs. Not seen anyone else actually. Except Ayesha, she is sleeping on a sofa in another room, don't know if they have had a barny or something?"

"Top gossip," she replied. The fireplace had a large black metal plated guard and behind it, dried flowers.

"Yep, it's all we have without radio and the telly I guess." Matt moved the guard away and tossed the dried flowers in the large grate; moving the vase they were in, to the side. There was a pile of logs in a recessed section of the fireplace; it looked like it was for effect rather than use. "We appear to have wood."

"Really," Hannah shrugged and groaned inwardly at the double American meaning to his words.

"Hey it's the apocalypse, bad jokes is all I got," he said in a terrible American New York accent.

"Is it the end of the world, you think?" Hannah knelt down as he handed her wood to put on the fire.

"Nah, I was only jesting. There have been things like this happening throughout history. Spanish flu killed millions in its day, the plague and other diseases. It's Mother Nature's way of decreasing the surplus population maybe, I dunno, I'm just a geography teacher and low-life scumbag." Matt stood up and went over to a magazine rack to pick up a copy of a glossy home interior design magazine. He knelt down again in front of the fireplace and began to rip pages off and crumple them up.

"Hey, don't do that. We all make mistakes, and I want us to be friends, for the baby's sake." Hannah gave his hand the briefest of squeezes.

"Friends," he repeated. "Better than dirty looks I guess. So you are keeping the baby, our baby?"

"Yes."

"Easy or hard decision?"

"I dunno, it sort of just sunk in. Not like there's an abortion clinic around or maybe even people to run it. I've lost so much I can't lose another blood relation. Sorry I should have talked to you about it really, but…" Hannah let the sentence hang.

"I'm the last person you want to talk to right. The cheating bastard who got his student pregnant when he should have been marrying his lesbian fiancée." Matt stuffed the rolled up paper into the cracks between the wood and next to the dried flowers.

"Life ain't easy anymore. But you are this baby's father, so we should make an effort to try and get along for his/her sake." Hannah touched her belly through the new jumper she found upstairs.

"Deal," Matt said and pulled a match from the large box. "You want the honours?"

"Nah, you go for it," Hannah smiled back at him.

"Okay." Matt struck the match and lit four different pieces of the magazine.

They had an anxious wait, but the dried flowers really caught, and the smoking logs joined in.

"Team parents," Matt said, holding a fist out to Hannah for her to bump.

She rewarded him with a hug instead.

It felt good to have her young body in his arms again. Matt tried to hide his broad smile as they parted.

"We have fire and light," Ayesha said from the doorway looking very worse for wear. "Well done you guys."

"You look how I feel," Selena piped up from the sofa as she woke up.

"You must feel well-drunk then babes," Ayesha said nearly stumbling over the sofa as she collapsed down on an armchair nearer the fire. "I'd kill for a cuppa tea and a kebab right now."

"What else would you kill for?" Charlie asked from the doorway with a severe tone in her voice.

"What's all this bloody yelling going on," Tony barged into the living room, where the rest of the group were shouting and bickering across the room at each other. "I can't hear myself drink." He said waving a bottle of whisky in his left hand. Ann followed at his tail.

"Ask these three," Charlie shouted at him, pointing to Brita, Ellie, and Ayesha.

"Okay, okay, calm your tits luv, what is going on? What have they done, formed a lesbo combo group without you?" Tony laughed at his own joke, but nobody else in the living room found it humorous.

"My mother's widow is accusing us three of being murderers, aren't you Charlie," Ayesha said in a calm, but simmering voice.

"Who have you lot supposed to have killed then?" Tony said back, as confused as his face showed.

"The owners of this house," Hannah said in a small voice.

"We know all that shit luv, Infected couple, had to be done, end of," Tony stated looking from one angry female face to the next. He was way out of his element here, it was true.

"But they weren't Infected were they," Charlie shot back at the three women standing across the room from her.

"We never said that they were," Brita replied in her low, calm voice.

"Fuck," Charlie spun round, her hands going into her hair. "So you aren't denying it then. You killed that couple in cold blood?"

"It wasn't like that, they threatened us first," Ellie shot back, tears streaming down her cheeks.

"What was it fucking like, then?" Charlie screamed at her.

Ellie shrunk back into Brita's arms.

"Let them speak please, and explain themselves," Selena said from the sofa.

"Come on then spill the bloody beans," Charlie raged.

"They opened the door, and the man had a shotgun pointed at us. He said he was going to kill us if we didn't leave his property. Then he pointed the shotgun at Ellie, I thought he was going to shoot her, so I shot him first. The wife ran at me with a little hand axe—"

"—So I stopped her," Ayesha said as calm as you like.

"You could have backed off and left," Charlie shouted at them.

"You weren't there," Ellie screamed with emotion at Charlie.

"We needed a place to stay, and nobody threatens my Ellie and gets away with it. I'd do it over again if it were to happen again." Brita held Ellie's sobbing body close as she faced Charlie down.

"Well then it's ok to kill people now is it cos they looked at your girlfriend in the wrong way. Is this what we have become in such a few short days, savages?"

"I'm not saying that at all. In situations like that, you have moments to react. Hesitation leads to death. What if he had shot Ayesha, would you still feel the same way?" Brita tried to reason with Charlie.

"You can never justify murder," Charlie said to the three she accused and then turned to Selena. "What are we going to do with them?"

"Why are you asking me?"

"Because you are a judge aren't you, we need judgement."

"I was a judge, but not at the moment."

"What are you then?"

"A survivor, like you and Ellie, and Ayesha and Brita. We all are," Selena said looking at her hands she kept ringing.

"So that makes it alright then, just shrug it off cos we are in a tight spot and the world is going to shit. Murder doesn't matter anymore." Charlie had rounded on Selena now, bending down to shout in her face.

"I'm not saying that we killed the Infected to survive, sometimes you have to assess the situation and all the mitigating circumstances before you give judgement."

"You are best suited to these circumstances. Why aren't you standing up for law and order, why aren't you raging inside at this like me?" Charlie jabbed a finger inches from Selena's nose.

"Because I'm a murderer too," Selena stood up and shouted into Charlie's red face.

"Blimey didn't see that one coming," Tony burped and then took another swig from his whisky bottle.

"What are you talking about?" It was Hannah's turn to jump up.

"Hey come on leave it now guys," Matt said trying to hold Hannah back and make peace.

"I knocked a woman off her bike with my car and left her to die in a ditch. I didn't call the police I just went home and put my car in the garage. When the flood hit my house, and I was trapped inside, and when I left days later to give myself in, the world had other problems to worry about. So, you see. I'm not in a position to judge anyone, anymore."

"How the mighty feminists have fallen?" Tony chided from the doorway.

"Fuck off," Selena and Charlie bellowed at him at once.

"Hey, I know when I'm not wanted. Why don't you form a circle and eat each other's hairy twats and work it all out, me and my straight wife are off to the kitchen."

"Come on." Ann urged her half drunken husband away before he could make matters even worse than they already were. She slipped under his arm with ease and led him away. It seemed to her than the high and mighty in the group, who always looked down on her and Tony, were not so clean living after all. Yet, she hoped they all stayed together, and the group did not fracture, she felt safer with them all. "Let's get you some food."

"I am starving," Tony burped again. Ann led him to the kitchen to see what there was to eat.

"What do we do now, to fix this?" Hannah said moving in-between all the different antagonists.

"Is there something to fix. We secured this house to keep the group safe, we took the risks so that everyone can benefit. You can look at us as bastards, for sure, but you need us." Brita said, in no mood for conciliation.

"You don't get it Brita, the ends don't justify the means," Charlie said, still angry, but not shouting.

"Maybe we should just leave this, get a good night's sleep and things might be better in the morning?" Matt said, moving closer to Hannah.

"Like we are going to listen to what a paedophile says," Ellie said venomously.

Matt looked crestfallen. "I never..."

"Come on Ellie, he maybe lots of things, but he isn't that," Hannah found herself defending him. "We never did anything before my sixteenth birthday."

"Just a child slut groomer, cheater, and bad teacher then, who got you pregnant," Ellie continued.

"What did you call me?" Hannah responded.

"Well look at you, the easy chavvy girl from a broken home, you probably got pregnant on purpose to live a life on benefits. Bet you didn't care he had a fiancée did you?" Ellie was furious, jabbing a finger at Hannah.

"Says the posh bird who cheated on him with a woman. You should take a look at yourself first before you judge others."

"That's enough," Matt said moving in-between them only to get a slap from Ellie intended for Hannah. "Fuck!"

"Stop it!" Ayesha screamed at the top of her lungs. "Matt s right, this ain't helping any. Let's just keep out of each other's way for tonight and sleep it off. I'm going to drink lots of water and then try and get some more sleep. Goodnight."

The rest of the group watched as Ayesha left them to their simmering rages and headed for the kitchen. Matt and Hannah left next, going upstairs with a candlestick, and this seemed to cause the rest of the group to silently disperse. Ellie and Brita went back to their room holding each other tightly. Charlie glared at Selena then went to find another room to sit alone. The very humid feeling living room was suddenly empty. She sat on the leather wingback chair closer to the fire all alone.

Her secret was out and so were many other tensions the group had been holding back. She wasn't sure how they were going to come back from this. Maybe getting it all out in the open was for the best. Selena held her palms out towards the fire.

"Let's see what tomorrow brings," she said to the dancing flames.

"How did your little chat go?" Tony asked from a stool in the kitchen.

"We heard the shouting, you okay luvvy?" Ann said as she dug through the cupboards for food.

Ayesha grabbed a bottle of water from the cooler by the fridge and left without speaking.

"Kids today eh," Tony said blowing out his lips. Ann was glad that he was in one of his good drunk moods tonight.

"Yep," was her only reply. She kept her head buried in the cupboard, to hide her tears from her husband. Her thoughts dwelled on her own children and grandchildren. Even if they did survive this outbreak, what lives would they have after?

Ellie took the rifle away from Brita and leant it against a set of drawers, then pushed her girlfriend towards the bed undressing them both in turn as they moved backwards.

"Are you okay?" Brita got out from between Ellie's passionate kisses.

"Fine, now shut up and make love to me." Ellie pushed her hard down onto the bed and held her down as her angry kisses continued.

Brita couldn't think of a better reply, so did just that.

"Well that could have gone better," Matt said as they reached the door to the bedroom Hannah had claimed.

"That fucking Ellie, how dare she have a pop at me, she don't know me." Hannah was still simmering.

"I think everyone was just a little overwrought and tired and very emotional," Matt said calmly.

"How can you be so chilled, she said some things to you too."

"I deserve it," he shrugged. "At least I didn't kill anyone."

"Yeah," Hannah whispered, recalling all of tonight's revelations. Selena's being the most shocking of all. She had looked up to her so much since they had found each other. Now she found out she has more flaws than anyone. She wasn't sure who she could trust or cling to anymore.

"Well, I guess I'd better let you rest," he said handing the candlestick over to her.

"What about you?" Hannah said waving the lit candlestick a little as he thrust his hands into his pockets.

"Ta-dah," he said pulling two candles from his pocket, "I have these."

"Cool."

"Night then," he said retreating two steps.

"You too."

"If you need anything," he thumbed behind him, "I'll be just down the landing."

Hannah smiled and opened her door and went inside.

Matt clicked his fingers and made for the dark room he had nabbed earlier. He sang a modern love song as he lit a candle and fixed it with hot wax onto an expensive cream wooden bedside table. He didn't care if it burnt it, wasn't his house. He slipped off his shoes and lay down on top of the covers. Putting his hands behind his head, he made himself comfortable and softly whistled the rest of the tune.

"Bide ya time Matthew," he said to the ceiling.

Charlie was still livid. The downstairs rooms were cold and looked unlived in. The laughing from the Gables in the kitchen didn't help, so she went upstairs to find her single room and wash before trying to get warm in bed.

The clothes she had on were not her own and the tight woollen pullover itched her arms. She closed the door and pulled the pullover off and headed into the en-suite bathroom. It was much darker inside than the bedroom, so she fetched the torch where Charlie had left it earlier on the bed. Switching it on she returned to the bathroom to wash her aching face. The tears and anger in her muscles were hurting down her jaw line. Putting the torch on a towel, she angled it into the sink and filled it up with cold water. She scratched her arm and then plunged her hands into the water and splashed it over her face. It was cold but very refreshing. She looked down at the sink to see the water was a tinged a little pink.

Charlie picked up the torch and shined it up onto her face and looked in the mirror above the white sink. Apart from being wet and slightly flushed she looked fine. She checked her hands, but they were ok. She scratched the itch again, as she frowned. She looked down at her fingertips that glistened red with blood. Pointing the torch to her upper forearm, Charlie soon found where the blood was oozing from.

"Oh, please God no," she whispered to the dark mirror.

CHAPTER SIXTEEN

A BAD NOTE

The next morning the sky above the big house was covered in a blanket of dark grey and black clouds. It had rained a little overnight, and the dark sky threatened more soon. The big house was isolated by the surrounding woods and the railway tracks that ran along outside. It was a good drive from anywhere local, even a village shop, but that's what had attracted the late owners to the property in the first place: seclusion.

Hannah was up first, with an urgent need to pee. This she assumed would only get worse as her pregnancy continued. As she sat on the loo, she wondered what it would feel like to give birth and what sort of world would be left to do it in. Hopefully, they would get the outbreak in check soon, and the floodwaters would eventually subside, making it easier to get around. The thought of giving birth without gas; drugs and doctors and nurses on standby scared the life out of her. But, that was something to worry about many months down the line. She and the rest of the group had to survive the outbreak first. To do that, they needed to pull together and not apart.

"We need to sort this before the shit gets out of hand," she said to the bathroom door.

Hannah dressed in warm borrowed clothes and wondered if she could find a sink to wash her own ones. She went downstairs to find the ground floor deserted, and the fire had died to cold grey ash. Hannah clicked her teeth as she copied Matt from last night by putting paper in the grate and covering it with wood. Then she looked around. She didn't have any matches to light the fire with.

"You may want to clear the old ash away next time for future reference. Do you need a light?"

Hannah stood up to see Selena had entered the living room and was brandishing a lighter at her.

"Cheers," Hannah said crisply and took the lighter and bent down to light the screwed up balls of magazine.

"Did you sleep well?"

Hannah rolled her eyes as the paper began to smoke and burn. She wasn't sure she was wide awake enough for pleasantries, after last night's revelations. Hannah did a well-practiced teen shrug and busied herself poking the fire with a set of coal tongs from a nearby brass bucket.

"I wouldn't poke it until it's a bit more well established, you know."

"What are you, the *fucking* fire police," Hannah muttered to herself.

"Did you say something; I couldn't quite hear?" Selena said moving closer.

"No, you're fine."

"Are you mad at me?"

"No, just disappointed, but I'm used to so-called adults letting me down. So hey, no worries eh." Hannah saw the wood was catching so stood up and wiped her hands on her jeans.

"I should have said something earlier to you and the group, but it's not the easiest thing to bring up in idle conversation."

"Like, hey I'll be your friend. Someone to admire, but hey I'm also someone who kills people by accident and doesn't admit to it." Hannah replied in a sing-song voice.

"I have no excuses, and I can't take back what I've done, Hannah, and when this is all over I will confess my crimes. Just let me keep you safe until we can find somewhere secure or where the infection hasn't reached. All I ask."

"I suppose, for the good of the group."

"You have a very old head on those young shoulders of yours, Hannah."

"Fire is lit, shall we make some breakfast for everyone and

try and cheer everyone up a bit."

"Yep, full stomach might help go a long way to heal last night's rifts. But I must warn you I'm not a great cook."

"That makes two of us. We might make things worse then." Hannah managed to smile at Selena.

Selena gave a tight-lipped smile as they headed for the kitchen.

Brita and Ellie were the next to turn up in the kitchen as Selena and Hannah were trying to find something to eat. There was plenty of cereal, but no fresh milk. Plenty of bread, but no working toaster.

Brita and Selena were holding hands and looked to Hannah the definition of a *loved-up* couple. Hannah was glad love still could exist in this terrifying crisis they found themselves in. She looked up from behind a low cupboard to see Matt enter the kitchen. He raised his eyebrows and hand at her in greeting and then went over to a far corner of the room. Hannah felt herself feel a little sorry for him. Sure, he was a weak man and a cheat, but he hadn't murdered anyone. He was the father of her unborn child, maybe she should give him a break. At least be his friend. It would be the best in the long run.

Brita and Selena were talking in hushed whispers like lovers do. They would chat and then kiss. Hannah looked back at Matt, he was staring at his shoes, looking embarrassed. She looked at his sad face, he had two ex's in one group, it must be hard for him.

"What's for fucking breakfast, I could eat a horse," Tony announced his arrival in the kitchen with his usual bellowing voice. Ann, as usual, followed in her husband's vast overbearing shadow.

"Whatever you can find?" Hannah replied.

"No bacon then, gymslip mum?" Tony said, looking pleased with himself for thinking up cutting things to say to people.

"Leave her alone," Matt and Selena said together.

"Well, I know why you are standing up for her, Mr. Soppy-Bollocks Grooming Teacher cos you knocked her up, but you Judge, what you going to do, run me over. Leave me for dead?"

"Tony, don't," Ann moved round to cajole her boorish husband into backing off a little. Tony stood his ground, legs apart, his tall, imposing frame the dominant thing in the kitchen.

"Anyone got any headache pills," Ayesha said, holding her head as she entered the kitchen. "And has anyone seen Charlie?"

Tony stared directly at Selena for a half a minute and then with a laugh headed for the door. "Wife, bring me some food."

Ann stopped following her husband. Stopped in her tracks, immediately embarrassed by her husband once again. She slipped back into the kitchen, eyes down.

"Why do you put up with that?" Selena said to her.

Ann didn't reply, she didn't have to justify her marriage to anyone, let alone a murderer. She looked at Brita and Ayesha, they were murderers too. She had nothing to be ashamed of compared to them. She moved over to the other side of the kitchen to look for something to feed Tony. She wondered, if by the end of this outbreak, that she might have to kill someone to survive. The thought turned her empty stomach.

"So, anyone seen Charlie?" Ayesha prompted again, pulling a large bottle of water from the not so cold fridge.

"Not this morning, no," Hannah said standing up from the cupboard holding two tins of peaches.

"Not seen hide nor hair of her since last night," Ann said.

"Where the bloody hell is she then?" Ayesha said, before taking a long swig of water.

"Checked her room?" Matt said, scratching the stubble forming on his chin.

"*Der'h*, first thing I did," Ayesha said, hydrating again.

"I'll help you look," Hannah said, putting down her peaches.

"Us too," Ellie said for her and Brita.

"I'm in." Matt raised his hand.

"Come on then, let's find Charlie. She might just have needed some space after last night," Selena said, clapping her hands together.

"Ayesha and I will start in the room Charlie used and upstairs," Hannah said, rubbing Ayesha's back.

"Ellie and I will check outside," Brita said, as they all left the kitchen.

"I'll look down here," Ann called after them.

The group split up and went about searching the house and grounds. Hannah took Ayesha's free hand and helped the hungover teen upstairs. Ayesha sipped water as they went along. They tried the room where she was supposed to have stayed the night.

"The bed doesn't look like it's been slept in. Unless she remade it this morning?" Hannah pointed out.

"Didn't notice that." Ayesha drank some more. "Saying that with me head thumping like this I ain't seeing much at all straight."

"Or this," Hannah said lifting an envelope from the bedside cabinet next to the made bed. It had Ayesha's name written on it.

"Give us that," Ayesha said putting down the water hard on the cabinet so it spilt a little on the clean, glossy white surface.

Hannah tried not to take offence when Ayesha snatched it from her hand and ripped the envelope open. Inside was a folded over piece of lilac writing paper, with Charlie's handwriting on both sides. Ayesha sat down on the bed with a bounce and began to read. Hannah could see Ayesha's face drop as she read down the first page and the tears brim and overflow from her eyes as she turned it over to continue reading Charlie's letter.

"No," was all Ayesha could croak as she sobbed her heart out.

"What does it say?" Hannah asked, her voice choked up just looking at the sadness and grief in her friend's face.

Ayesha said nothing. She just held the letter out to Hannah in a trembling hand. Hannah took it delicately like it was an ancient Egyptian papyrus. Ayesha turned and pulled her legs up onto the bed. She buried her tears into the pillow and gave out wailing sobs that were heart-breaking to hear.

Hannah was torn between comforting her friend, or reading the letter. In the end, she fudged it and sat on the bed. One hand rubbing Ayesha's hitching side, the other holding and reading the letter:

My Dearest Brave and Beautiful Ash,
I don't think I've ever written to you before, unless it was notes

to school to help you bunk off PE because of "period pains." It seems strange to write one now, I've almost forgotten how to write in this modern age. I want to tell you that even though I did not give birth to you, that you always felt like my own child. Thank you for letting me be your second mum, I know having two Lesbian Mums at school must have been hard at times. I don't think my body could have made a more perfect and beautiful child than you anyway. It was a pleasure watching you grow up into a funny, but wild, adult. I know I had it easier than your mum, cos we were mates and I let you get away with murder. I loved you as I loved your mum, our beloved Pam, so, so much.

Now the hard part. I need you to be stronger than ever before and rely on the good people in the group to help you through this. I forgive you everything, every harsh word or angry word or anything else you did. You need to be strong to survive now, but please don't lose the soft, funny side of Ash that I love so well. You have lost your mum and Piers so quickly, try to keep your shit together now, promise me.

Here goes. I have the Red Death infection. I spotted it last night. I've disinfected everything I can remember touching, but be careful, everyone should check themselves. I know it's a death sentence and even worse I could become one of those mindless things and hurt you all. So I'm leaving before anyone else gets ill, or God (that's a joke) forbid I hurt anyone else. DO NOT follow me, I'll find someplace quiet to be with my thoughts. My last ones will be of you and your mum.

I'm hoping my atheist side is wrong, and I see your mum soon. I will send her your regards.

Be stronger than ever before, my lovely child.

Love you forever.

Your second mum, Charlie xxx

Hannah had joined Ayesha in crying. She put the farewell letter on the side and spooned Ayesha close. They were still there half an hour later when Matt and Selena found them.

Brita chewed her bottom lip and looked around the woods surrounding the Big House. "This is pointless, we will never find Charlie in this, even if she came this way."

"A little bit further, I want to see where this road leads anyway. We might need it when we leave."

"She could be back at the house as we speak," Brita whined, adjusting the rifle strap on her shoulder.

"Just over this little rise, then I'll let you kiss me, and we'll head back, okay?"

"How can I ever resist you?" Brita moved into Ellie's waiting arms and kissed her lips.

"You can't," Ellie said between breathless kisses on the top of the rise.

"Good," Brita said pulling Ellie into a chest crushing emotional hug. Then she spotted a ladder leant up against a large oak down the slope below. It stuck out: the grey metal against the brown and green of the trees. "Oh no."

"What's wrong?" Ellie asked turning to see where Brita was looking. She too, saw the ladder and then the short rope and then the red partly flayed looking body hanging by the neck from it.

CHAPTER SEVENTEEN

DEPARTING

They dug a shallow grave and on Ayesha's insistence, burnt the body where it lay. She didn't want Charlie's brave end to infect anyone else. Everyone turned up, even the Gables. Tony was silent for once, and everyone, apart from him and Ayesha, cried.

The tear well had dried up for Ayesha. Her eyes felt like someone had rubbed them with grit, and she could not cry anymore. She stood numb, on the top of the rise, watching the body of her second mother burn. The rest of the group stayed with her in silent reverence to her and Charlie.

It would have been easy to die in bed hoping against hope that you would not succumb to the Red Death, but she had taken her death into her own hands. She went out on her own terms, and even Tony could see how brave a decision that must have been. No goodbyes, just grab a ladder walk into the dark woods alone and end it all.

The group parted after the flames began to die, leaving Ayesha alone on the rise, with Hannah a respectful few steps behind. The rest of the group split up, most returning to the house. Selena caught sight of something through the trees, and Brita and Ellie went with her to investigate. The others went back to the house and began to pack and find water and food for the next part of their journey to Farnborough. Nobody spoke more than two words to each other.

As Hannah comforted Ayesha as best she could, Selena led the other two women north through the line of trees to where something glinted in the weak sunlight. They came out of the woods to find an overgrown towpath and a large canal flowing east and west before them. It was so close to the house up and down a rise, they wondered how they missed it. It was hidden, with deep thick woods bordering on each side.

"Hey look." Ellie pointed down the canal to where a brightly painted narrowboat was moored.

"This is good," Selena said almost to herself and then jogged down the towpath towards it. She felt better, but not up to running speed yet.

"What are we doing, looking for supplies?" Brita called after her.

"No, we are looking for a way out of here, that won't tire out my weary old legs," Selena cried back with a breathless laugh in her voice from somewhere.

Ellie and Brita exchanged bemused glances as they hurried after her. They caught up as Selena bent double, hands on knees trying to breathe and not throw up at the same time. The narrowboat was bright gloss green along the hull, bow, stern and cabin edgings, with red on the side panels with flowery golden designs. A weathered blue cover was over the stern of the boat. It looked unoccupied, but in good condition to Selena. She and David had taken a few narrowboat holidays when they were younger and could not afford to fly abroad. She hoped he was still out there somewhere with his new family safe on the river away from all this madness.

The banks of the canal had risen over the towpath in places and the area around the stern of the boat was awash with deep muddy pools, with islands of tall grass.

"It looks so pretty, like *Rosie and Jim's* narrowboat," Ellie cooed, recalling a childhood memory.

"Rosie and Jim?" Brita looked at her, bemused, maybe it was some of Ellie's relatives.

"Children's TV show with puppets, they used to live on a narrowboat like this. Do you think it will go?" Ellie asked Selena excitedly.

"If we can get onboard," Selena replied looking at the submerged concrete mooring and the deep dark gap between the canal and the boat.

"Don't want to expose ourselves to fresh water, it could be polluted with the virus," Brita warned.

"We need something like a plank to walk across." Ellie looked at the high grass and trees, but could see nothing suitable.

"Or a ladder," Selena said solemnly.

"Do you want to say something, any words?" Hannah asked, walking up to stand beside Ayesha in her grief.

"And say what, Charlie didn't believe in God and who can blame her."

"Then say nice things about her, special memories, like a memorial to her life, don't have to be religious and that."

"I dunno if I can. She was my special second mum, and I loved her. Now she is dead, like my mum and like Piers. Ain't going to care or love again Han, it just hurts too much." Ayesha looked at her new friend. Her eyes were tired and had dark rings, but there were no tears.

"Maybe in time?"

"What time, any of us could get this shitty infection, Charlie is proof of that. We are all on borrowed time. We might as well just sit down and wait for it to happen."

"I can't do that, and nor can you. I've lost all the family I've ever known, and this little bump will need a cool kick-arse aunty if you are up for the job." Hannah took Ayesha's hand and held it to her tummy. She knew there wasn't much to feel, but she had to get Ayesha believing in life again.

"I'll try, but no one can make any promises anymore. I'll be here for you as long as I can. Is that good enough?"

"Yes," Hannah said, and they embraced, united in their loss.

"So what do we do now?" Ayesha whispered into Hannah's ear.

"We keep on moving, fighting and surviving I guess."

Ayesha left the embrace first but turned to see it was because Selena, Brita, and Ellie were returning up the rise.

"Hi, Ayesha. We think we've found a way out of here, but we need to borrow the ladder if that's ok?" Selena asked with as much tact as she could muster.

"Yeah, sure."

"What do you need a ladder for?" Hannah asked the other women.

"Come and see, you'll bloody love it," Ellie said, her face lit up.

"You want us to do what?" Ann shot back, after being told the plan, she hated the sea, rivers and even got seasick on a pedalo once in Marbella.

"It will save us walking along train tracks and flooded roads. Think of it: a boat in a flood is the ideal solution to this. I found a map of the waterways onboard. The canal runs right past Farnborough. We'd be mad not to do this." Selena explained to her in the living room of the Big House.

"Have you started it up, checked for leaks?" Matt piped up. He too was unsure of this new form of transport.

"Yes, and we have plenty of fuel and clean water and electricity if we need it. Heating, hot showers."

"Will it fit us all?" Ann frowned, not giving up on her reservations.

"Yes, it's sixty feet long. There are three beds and a booth like couch around a table that could sleep two. We can take turns in sleeping and driving the boat."

"What do you think Tone?" Ann looked down at her seated husband, who had been unusually quiet so far.

"I think it makes sense. I'm fucking sick of walking and having soggy socks."

And that was it. With Tony onboard the decision-making process was over. The groups split up and readied themselves and grabbed as many supplies as they could. Everyone was glad to leave the house, in the end, making the short trip down to the canal. They found some jerry cans in the garage and siphoned out the diesel from the Range Rover. Taking as much clothes and bedding; water, drinks, and food as they could, they soon had the narrowboat stocked to the rafters. The boat wasn't too wide, but the modern interior and the length made sure there was space for everyone. The Gables claimed the only double bed, but the others weren't too put out, at least they were out of sight and mind that way. With the other single bed and the

L-shaped couch, they could take turns to sleep and keep the boat running. Only Selena had experience of narrowboats before, so she took the helm.

"So we ready for the off?" Selena asked Ellie, Brita and Hannah, who were outside with her, on or around the stern.

"Yes," Ellie replied, who, apart from Selena, was in her element. She had never been on a narrowboat before, but her dad had owned a pleasure cruiser on the Thames for years. She immediately became Selena's First Mate.

Brita untied the last mooring rope and used the ladder to cross on-board. The boat began to drift out into the middle of the canal, and Selena disengaged the gearbox and opened the throttle slightly. She closed the pressure release valve and turned the ignition key to I. Then hitting mid-stream pushed the throttle forward with her left hand, the right on the tiller keeping the boat straight.

"And off we go," Selena said as the rotor gained purchase underwater and the narrowboat began to head west along the Basingstoke Canal. The views were little more than the water ahead and the woods on either side. The new crew of the Narrowboat did not mind; they could think of nowhere safer from the Infected crazies than the middle of a canal.

"What's she called?" Hannah asked Selena as she steered the boat.

"The *Ramses Two*," Selena replied. She had spotted the name on the stern of the boat earlier.

"Godspeed the intrepid crew of the *Ramses Two*," Ellie said in a booming manly voice. Brita and Ellie sat on the roof of the boat while Hannah stood next to Selena trying to learn the nuances of narrowboat steering. In the sky, the sun poked through the clouds and sent warming rays of light over the narrowboat. The four women outside could not help but smile as the sun warmed their faces and hands.

Inside, Tony and Ann lay on the double bed. Tony was already asleep and snoring. Ann felt okay if she lay flat on her back and didn't open her eyes. Matt was in the kitchen area making toast, now they had electricity and gas and teas for everyone if he could find enough mugs. Ayesha sat at the table that easily could sit six, all alone. She stared out the small window and watched the woods go by on either side.

"Goodbye, Second Mum," she whispered.

They chugged along quicker than walking speed and without the effort.

"Why didn't we think of this before, flood and boats, so much better ways to travel," Brita said lying on a towel next to Ellie as the full sun beat down on the only boat on the canal. They passed nothing and saw no signs of life from the roof of the narrowboat apart from the odd wood pigeon and squirrel.

"Not sure. Glad, though, it's like our honeymoon," Ellie giggled and kissed Brita unawares on the lips, as her eyes were closed against the glare.

"Tea for the workers?" Matt cried coming out of the cabin door holding a tray of five tea mugs and a bowl of sugar lumps and spoons.

Hannah hopped forwards off the side of the boat to help distribute the teas around.

"Well done, you." She smiled at him.

Matt smiled back. "I aim to be more useful now."

"Good start," she said, and they clinked their tea mugs together.

After the loss of Piers and Charlie, the narrowboat, sunshine, and quiet canal seemed a Godsend and a relief from their recent losses. Something seemed to be going their way at last. Matt stood next to Hannah as they sipped their tea. The *Ramses Two* passed a half sunken older looking narrowboat thirty minutes into their journey. It reminded them of the perils of the floods but did not dampen their sunny moods.

Ellie began to sing a recent pop song about love and sunshine, and they were surprised at what a lovely soulful tone she had to her voice. Everything was going fine for the present until they reached their first test: a lock.

They had travelled for forty-five minutes like they were on a boating holiday. Tea and the sunshine had lifted their mood. The first lock was exciting and seemed less of a hindrance. Selena left Ellie in charge of the boat as she and the others tried to figure out the workings of the lock. They had to find a skeleton key and winder on a belt hanging up near the engine room to really get things moving. Tony, becalmed after his restful nap, came up to help. He was loud and pushy, but his sheer strength in moving the lock gates all by himself was definitely required.

Matt felt slightly inadequate as he could not manage it, so went and made the big man a cup of tea as suggested. The first lock navigated, Selena gave quick lessons to Hannah and Brita on the finer points of steering a narrowboat. To their surprise, Tony rolled up his sleeves and drank his tea in silence. He too was enjoying the trip, and the sunshine and using his strength made his caveman brain contented.

The next lock came sadly ten minutes later. Then twelve minutes later two more locks in quick succession. Then within a mile another seven locks, which dampened everyone's spirits and even tired Tony out. They moored in the middle of the canal after the last of the seven locks and Ellie cooked up some soup and toasted some stale bread for everyone. Everyone but Ayesha and Ann wolfed down the hot food. Ann was still feeling sick if she even sat up and Ayesha was in the single bedroom and not in the mood for food or company. Hannah had tried to persuade her to eat, but Ayesha just showed her her back. So Hannah left her to her thoughts and rejoined the others. They were tired out by the locks, but it also bonded them as a group again, given a task. Even Tony was in a good mood, telling bawdy jokes; it was at least better than him taking the mickey out of everyone. They felt safe and secure in their little life raft away from the death and infection going on around them.

That feeling did not last very long.

CHAPTER EIGHTEEN

DEAD WATER

After lunch they continued on down the Canal, it was another fifteen minutes until they reached another deserted lock, but after that, it was plain sailing for a while. The series of many locks in close proximity seemed to be behind them, and Ellie alone on the tiller dared to increase the speed for a time.

They had just passed under a road bridge and ahead on the right bank was a row of houses on the river. Most had docks that were submerged by the swollen canal. Some had rowing boats, others cruisers moored nearby. More than half of them were sunk, one was wrapped around a tree by its twisted mooring rope. A punt was drifting near the middle of the canal, so Ellie steered the narrowboat towards the left bank a little. Even then she clipped the side of the punt with a loud bump and sent it spinning in lazy circles towards the right bank near the houses. It probably saved their lives.

Ellie heard them before she saw them.

They came screaming and splashing along a flooded decking area at one end of a garden. At least twelve or more Infected wailing and roaring with pain and anger as they ran as fast as their flesh wasted bodies would allow.

"Brita," Ellie screamed trying to keep the narrowboat steady, but she pushed the throttle too hard to escape and over steered so the *Ramses Two* veered into an overhanging old willow on the left bank.

She tried to cut her speed and correct her course but just made it worse. She drifted into the weeds, roots and branches of the willow and stalled the engine in panic. The narrowboat jolted and stopped dead.

The Infected ran on and fell splashing into the swollen leaf-strewn canal. Some jumped, with their lipless mouths open showing too many teeth. Of the dozen that dove in after the boat, half did not resurface. Three more floundered and splashed about in circles while the other three seemed to remember the art of swimming and made a bee-line for the *Ramses Two*.

Brita, carrying the automatic rifle appeared at the hatch doorway first. She saw the fear on Ellie's face and went to comfort her. Ellie had one hand to her mouth the other she waved frantically for Brita to turn around and see the danger they were in. She turned to see the Infected swimming their way and closing fast on where they were stuck on the left bank. She did not flinch at their disfigured faces, she fired a long rapid burst of bullets into the water, hitting all three of the Infected swimmers in the back. One rolled over and roared in pain, so she shot it again in the head. The other two were just floating face-down corpses in the canal.

Tony, Matt, and Selena appeared on the very tightly crowded stern.

"Matt, get Ellie down below," Brita shouted behind her, as she fired a single shot, taking down an Infected who was trying to clamber up on the punt. It head-butted the side of the punt and then slid under the dirty waters.

Matt ushered the near hysterical Ellie away, as Selena took the controls of the narrowboat. Tony stood with an eight-foot-long pole, with a brass hook he had found on hooks down in the cabin.

Another Infected had found her swimming action and was making doggy paddle efforts to get to the narrowboat. Brita aimed the rifle at her.

"Save your ammo, I got this bitch," Tony said to her. Brita frowned and stepped aside. Looking like Captain Ahab Tony plunged the spike of the pole deep into the head of the swimmer and pushed down with all his might. A jerk from the boat, as Selena reversed it, made him wobble for a frightening second, but then he hauled the pole sharply back, and the Infected woman did not bob back up, dead, for at least three seconds. He and Brita had to grab the roof of the boat as Selena reversed it back out of the weeds and willow. Brita and Tony kept an eye on the other splashing Infected as they reversed clear of the willow. Selena steered the boat to a straight course and then gunned the throttle forwards. They waited as the boat tried to get traction, like a cat on a polished wooden floor and they were off again.

Hannah and Ayesha appeared at the front of the narrow-boat, looking around, concerned. There were a few more baying Infected in the gardens of the other houses as they sped past, but none tried the kamikaze water attack again. They were soon into a narrow overgrown section of the canal with trees over-hanging on both banks, and the houses and Infected were left behind.

Everyone on deck let out a long sigh of relief. Selena steered the narrowboat as Tony ducked down low to head back inside with his wet pole.

"That was too close," Selena stated.

"For sure," Brita said, sitting down near her to check her ammo clip. She had only three rounds left. She switched to sin-gle fire, put on the safety and hoped nothing else would require her rifle skills today. "Will you be okay here? I need to check on Ellie."

"Looks quiet now, you go," Selena replied.

Hannah waved from the bow and Selena gave her a quick thumbs up. The new rule was no one steers alone without a lookout on the bow section.

The next section of the canal grew tighter with grass and trees, and she had to slow down to a crawl to keep the nar-rowboat in the middle of the decreasing width. The canal bent south, and Selena slowly eased it around the tight bend. What she saw next, vexed her, and she brought the narrowboat to a dead stop and weighed anchor at both ends.

Everyone came up on deck, and Hannah and Ayesha walked over the roof of the cabin to join them all. Even Ann came up on deck, as they were relatively still, nibbling a ginger biscuit like when she was pregnant and feeling sick. Selena consulted the

Basingstoke canal map and found where they were. The *Ramses Two* was anchored in a broad part of the canal. To the right was an ancient looking grey stone bridge that led into a lake and ahead round the bend was a lower looking red/orange brick bridge which didn't show much beyond.

"Okay red bridge leads on down the canal and eventually round to Farnborough, the other leads to a lake. So, if there aren't any objections, continue on I say." Selena, the captain of the ship in this instance, got no objections.

"Carry on," Hannah said, just to be polite.

"Weigh anchor," Matt said because he had always wanted to say it and had never had the opportunity before. He moved to pull up one and Ayesha the other.

They were about to when two Chinook helicopters roared overhead two hundred feet up heading west. Ayesha, Ann, and Ellie waved frantically at them, but the large helicopters did not deviate from their flight paths.

"Didn't see us," Tony said in a smug voice.

"At least we know the military are still around," Selena said, trying to be more upbeat.

"You better get this old tub moving then," Tony said, ducking down low again to go below. Ann followed him below before her sea legs left her again. Selena stuck two fingers up at their retreating backs and urged the *Ramses Two* on down the canal and under the red brick bridge.

They passed some large buildings to their left and some houses that seemed deserted of any kind of life apart from a black cat on the lawn licking at its paw. More houses sped past on either side. Ayesha and Hannah kept a wary eye out on each bank from the bow again. Houses gave way to a large concrete bank where two other narrowboats were moored. They saw no signs of life, only death. A dead man, ravaged by the Red Death lay slumped against the tiller of his boat *Rebus III*. They passed under a bridge with large houses on either bank before disappearing again into deep cover, with thick woods on either side. The canal was wide, but once again there was nothing to see but trees, which made Selena feel a lot more content. Apart from a path cut through the woods for telephone and electricity poles, there was nothing much to see but birds and squirrels on the trunks of trees. Ellie with Brita as her protective shadow came up on deck, as the sun dappled through the leaves. She took the tiller for a while, giving Selena a toilet and biscuit break. Brita stayed within two inches of her girlfriend this time.

Apart from passing a pond with all sorts of ducks and swans on the one side, Ellie's stint on the helm was much less eventful than the last. She slowed as they passed under a metal pedestrian bridge into an area where several narrowboats were moored in special docks on either side. A large pub was on the left bank, and the canal tripled in width. Ellie wished they could stop for a pint, but felt safer just chugging past. Getting to Farnborough airfield without stopping was their goal.

Hannah brought two cans of Pepsi she found in a pack in a cupboard near the sink and handed one to Ayesha as they sat on the bow of the boat as joint lookouts.

"Cheers," Ayesha said popping the tab and taking a long drink. She hadn't realised she was thirsty until Hannah had brought her the can. She had just been watching the sun glint across the water as they ploughed through it. She looked at Hannah and smiled in spite of how down she felt. "So, fucked ya teacher eh, now that's something even I never did, one up on me gurl."

Hannah looked back down the cabin and then closed the angled doors so they could lean on them and have some privacy to talk.

"So, spill?"

"Spill what?" Hannah blushed and drank her Pepsi to cover her flushed cheeks.

"What was it like with sir?"

Hannah looked at Ayesha and smiled wickedly. "It was hot, cos we were a dirty sexy secret affair thing, well at the time I thought that."

"And now?"

"And now I'm up the duff from an adult who cheated on his lesbian fiancée with a student, and I think he's just a saddo bastard."

"Not tempted then?" Ayesha nudged her biting her bottom

lip and fluttering her eyelids. "It's not like you have to worry about getting pregnant."

"I dunno, he is trying to be nice. It's a hard one." Hannah shrugged.

"Hard is gooooood," Ayesha purred. "Anyway, apart from ten ton Tony or me following in my mums' footsteps, your choices are limited."

"Thanks," Hannah said but didn't mean it.

"Don't worry, I'll look after you," Ayesha said and put her arm around Hannah's neck.

"You turned fast."

"Shuddup."

Hannah put her arm around Ayesha's waist, and they put their heads together.

"This world is fulla shit," Hannah said.

"And shits," Ayesha said.

"You've got me."

"And you got me." The conversation ended there, and they just watched the *Ramses Two* plough through the water making waves that bounced over the swollen banks. For a time at least the world around them was peaceful and bore no immediate dangers.

The day wore on, and this section of the canal was devoid of the cumbersome locks. The width of the canal grew wider, and they passed through two large lakes. Both were silent worlds filled with bobbing ducks, geese and even herons. The sun was high and warm now, and Ayesha and Hannah felt dozy and wished for sunglasses or/and hats. The canal seemed a holiday away from the death and chaos of the world around them.

Selena watched from the stern steering the narrowboat with an expertise that she had hadn't used for over twenty or more years. Maybe after all this she could sell her sunken home and buy a sailing boat and travel around the world alone. Either that or the grey bars and walls of a woman's prison. She shook the rain, death, and darkness from her mind. She had to enjoy moments of calm like this. Charlie's sudden infection and suicide had taught them that death could reach out its cold, bony fingers and stop their beating hearts at any second.

As they passed through another lake, screams of fear could be heard from behind the trees and hedged line right bank. Brita and Matt appeared up on deck, but they could only hear the terrified cries, a sudden scream and then nothing. Matt went back below after five minutes, but Brita sat cross-legged on the roof of the cabin, the automatic rifle resting across her thighs.

The canal narrowed again, and the bushes, trees, and grass choked the view on both banks. Brita wasn't sure if she felt better that their boat trip was passing trouble spots with ease, or nervous of what the close woods could hide. The leaves and branches became so dense for a while they formed a roof over the canal as they passed, shutting out most of the warming sunlight. Without it, the deck of the narrowboat felt cold, and the only sound was the chug of the engine as they passed through the shadows.

Everyone was glad to exit the darkness as the sunlight covered them again. They passed under a bridge and a small white cruiser with a streak of vivid blood splashed up one side. It wasn't two more minutes when they passed two dead bodies in life jackets stuck in the reeds on one side of the canal.

Another large pub on the left bank signaled a return to a more suburban setting with gardens backing up on each side. The houses looked either boarded up or empty, some had Infected roaming on the tended lawns aimlessly seeking people to either kill or pass on the Red Death that coursed through their veins and rotted their skin off.

Five minutes later, they saw a teen girl and a boy of four sitting on a flat shed roof; supplies scattered around them. Selena had slowed the *Ramses Two* to a stop to wave them over to rescue them. Ayesha and Hannah urged the Asian girl and the frightened white child down. They finally scrambled down, only to be jumped by four Infected waiting in the bushes for them. Brita stood up to fire, but the two of them were bitten and torn apart before she could even get off a shot. There was little point wasting her three remaining rounds on revenge. Selena throttled up and away from the bank. They did not try again to save anyone they saw that day, however much they cried for help. It was too dangerous for either party.

Ayesha and Hannah went below after that, crushed by what had happened. Ellie joined Brita, bringing coffee for the deck crew. Matt volunteered to keep watch at the front of the narrow-boat alone. He had found some binoculars in a cupboard below, so he scanned the way ahead as much as the trees and homes lining the canal would allow. The houses and warehouses on the flooded left bank soon gave way to submerged towpaths on either side with close trees, tall grass once more.

After a while, Selena let Ellie take over so she could go below and have a lie-down and a break. Ayesha and Hannah were dozing, heads on each other's shoulders in the booth around the table. Ann was in the main bedroom and Tony in the only armchair reading a fishing magazine he had found. Selena went to the cramped loo and then lay down on the single bed, glad to be alone for a while.

Above her Brita, Ellie and Matt looked over the side in shock as the canal passed over the flooded four lanes of an A road below. The low road was sunken from the flooded lakes and wetlands that surrounded it. Hundreds of cars, lorries and vans were caught in an endless traffic jam. Infected roamed the chest high water, searching the vehicles for trapped people. Ellie wiped a tear and looked ahead to concentrate on the narrow part of the aqueduct type bridge they had to traverse. She saw Matt lower the binoculars and wipe his eyes on the cuffs of his blue pullover. Only Brita kept her crystal blue eyes on the road until it was lost from view.

The flooding was deep and covered the banks and sur-rounding fields and industrial estates. Ellie was so glad of the narrowboat. The railway tracks would have been a nightmare of cold and wet feet and legs if they had stuck to them. In a dangerous flooded, Infected world, the best place was above the polluted waters. The air was still and almost humid for the time of year and the area silent as the grave. They had to hope that the helicopters they had seen this morning were not a false dawn and that not far ahead civilisation, the authorities, and the military were waiting to protect them all.

Brita was the first to tip her head skywards as something

roared like an industrial lion. Then they heard a sonic boom and the scream of metal tearing itself apart. An upside down Hercules transport jet with its tail missing roared over the boat at a terminal velocity; raining burning bodies in its wake. It cleared the narrowboat by fifty feet rendering Ellie, Brita and Matt temporarily deaf from the screaming engines. Burning fuel, fuselage and body part splashed into and around the canal ahead. Matt dived down, and Brita jumped into Ellie's arms as they tumbled to the hard deck.

The Hercules engines and metal screamed once more, as did the pilots inside, as it crashed into the airfield only a mile away. The explosion, noise, fire and smoke was enormous, rocking the narrowboat as it drifted into the right bank. Then there was a null void of noise, and they heard the screaming. It took a moment or two to realise it was they who were making the noise.

CHAPTER NINETEEN

FARNBOROUGH

It was nearly dusk by the time they had reached the outskirts of the airfield at Farnborough. Selena was at the tiller. Only Tony was on deck at the prow of the boat with his pole, pushing bits of bodies, and burning wreckage out of the way, just incase they caught on the rotor. The canal was no longer silent, all around them explosions and noise of battle could be heard. Artillery and attack helicopters roared overhead, not even seeing the narrowboat.

A war seemed to be raging on either side of the banks, but apart from the noise and the odd ball of flame, the occupants of the *Ramses Two* were cocooned in their narrow little waterway. The canal map showed they were squeezed in-between the vast army town of Aldershot and Farnborough airfield. They were just turning a bend that showed glimpses of the airfield to their right; when a flight of Chinooks and other smaller army helicopters took off on mass from the airfield. They flew up and past with a sound like a swarm of hornets and bees at least twenty strong.

The battle, it seemed, was over.

They passed under a metal bridge and looked right. Selena slowed the narrowboat to a stop on the right-hand bank but did not drop anchor. Tony looked back at her across the boat in shock. Farnborough airfield was burning.

Not in one place, but many. The Hercules had crashed into the control tower destroying both. Other buildings and aircraft were aflame, the surrounding buildings, hangers, and homes were also ablaze. The place was a burning inferno everywhere they looked, making their eyes water with the glare and pungent smoke.

The rest of the group came up on deck to witness the burning of another dream of sanctuary. A cargo plane exploded across the runway from them, causing them to all flinch down. There was no rescue to be had here, no safe haven. The military had left it behind, in a tactical retreat. Then Matt spotted them, with his binoculars. Fifty or so figures staggering from the flames in all areas of the airfield, trying to escape the fire. At first, he thought they were survivors, but when they jumped upon a crawling injured man, he knew what they were. Survivors of the Red Death: Infected.

"Infected, fucking loads of them," he warned the others, lowering the binoculars.

"Let's go?" Brita urged Selena.

Selena grabbed the tiller again and throttled the narrowboat slowly away from the right bank.

"Where to though?" Ann asked, feeling seasick and crushed at the same time.

"Anywhere but bloody here will do," Tony shouted as some of the Farnborough Infected spotted them and dashed off the lit airfield towards them.

They were away and behind the cover of a line of trees before any of the Infected reached the road near the banks of the canal. Brita hugged Ellie close and kissed her forehead. Ayesha and Hannah clasped hands, even Tony put a comforting arm around Ann's shoulders. Soon the flames were visible only as glowing smoke above the enclosing trees. The *Ramses Two* disappeared into the shadows, and the Infected lost interest in pursuit.

Selena had no idea where they were heading, except away from the carnage and burning airfield. She had not looked beyond Farnborough, a planning mistake she would not make again. Contingencies and backup plans were now the order of the day. She switched on the lamps on the front of the narrowboat to see where they were heading, deeper into the darkness and leaving the flames of the airfield behind.

The light at the front of the narrowboat helped, but Selena jolted each bank twice as night fell. They found a wide isolated stretch of the canal and dropped anchor in the centre, hoping no other boats would come along in the night. They hadn't seen another moving craft on the canal since they had been on it, so it was an acceptable risk. They battened down the hatches and locked and shuttered the windows to keep the *Ramses Two* as dark as possible from outside prying eyes.

They used candles and lamps for light, trying to save the electricity the engines provided. They cooked up a hearty meal but knew they needed diesel, candles, food and more water, now their journey on the narrowboat had been extended. Selena knew how to run and steer the narrowboat, but had no idea how long the diesel would last. They would have to stop and scavenge for supplies pretty soon, finding a safe, not too flooded place to do that would be fun.

She checked the engine room but wasn't sure which gauge meant what. She headed back into the long main room with everyone else, figuring she could try and find a manual in a drawer somewhere. But, Hannah grabbed her arm and led her down to the bench seat she had vacated and poured her a glass of wine brought from the Big House.

"You deserve it, and anyway I'm off the hard stuff now," Hannah said, patting her tummy.

Selena squeezed her hand and gulped the wine down in three goes. She looked to see everyone was staring at her. "Well, it's been a long bloody day."

"But what do we do now?" Matt asked leaning on the head-rest behind Hannah.

"Everywhere we go, it's all death and destruction," Ellie said, cuddling close to Brita.

"We keep going," Tony stated.

"But where to?" Ann piped up.

"In the words of Churchill, we keep buggering on," Selena said, pulling the folded canal map from her inside coat pocket. She opened it carefully and laid it on the table, it was already a bit dog-eared when they came onboard. Her finger followed the flow of the canal past Farnborough to a kink in the river, where she stabbed her forefinger. "We are here now. If we follow the canal along we can get to this place, called Greywell. It's near another RAF base, we could try for that or head to the coast, Southampton, Portsmouth, hope the Navy can help us escape or try to get a boat to the Isle of Wight or France."

"Why the bloody hell would we want to go to Frog-land, we need to stay here and fight," Tony boomed.

"Let's just get to the end of the canal and figure it out from there," Matt suggested.

"But we need a plan, not to drift along and see what happens." Hannah glanced up at her former lover and teacher.

"Ellie and I would try for a boat to Europe and get back to Denmark," Brita pointed out.

"I think we are safer on the narrowboat," Ann said, taking a sip of her wine.

"For the moment, I agree. Yet if we see an opportunity to safely leave the canal before it runs out we take it; agreed?" Selena said, looking at the faces of the group.

"Agreed," Brita said, and everyone else murmured their approval or nodded.

"Stay on here as long as we safely can or the diesel lasts, see what happens tomorrow and keep our plans fluid. If nothing safe or secure appears we take this boat to the end of the line and then try for the RAF base and if that's compromised, for the coast again, flooding permitting." Selena reiterated her thoughts.

"Yep, now budge up. Ann and I are going to get some sleep," Tony said in the least confrontational tone they had heard him use since they met him. Selena thought, he and his barbed mind must be tired. Hannah and Ayesha had to get up to let them out.

"Night, bitches," he said as he and Ann made for the double bedroom, dispelling that train of thought. The rest of the group frowned, but said nothing back, they too were exhausted after today.

"Who sleeps where then?" Matt asked the most pertinent question of the day.

"I think Captain Selena should get the bed and Brita and Ellie can bunk here. Guess the rest of us fight for the armchair,"

Hannah gave a tired laugh, but there was little joy in it.

"But you are pregnant, maybe you should get the bed," Selena said to Hannah.

"I'm hardly showing, we are warm and dry here, and I've slept in worse places since this all happened," Hannah said, getting up from the booth-table.

"Too tired to argue," Ayesha yawned. "Let's see what spare blankets we have about the boat."

Hannah took the armchair in the end and Ayesha and Matt the floor, with picnic blankets and cushions to give them some comfort. They doused the lights and settled down for their first night on the narrowboat. It took a while for all of them to get to sleep. Bad memories, fire and death, plus the unsettling movement of the boat in the water made it difficult to drift off.

In the end, they all got differing amounts of sleep in different stages.

Sadly, they were all awakened by heavy rain and high winds just after dawn. They found that the *Ramses Two* was not the driest boat around its doorways, and a grey gloom hung over the crew as they had tea and breakfast.

They ate and drank in silence, hoping the rain might ease off, but it didn't. After an hour, they could not delay their departure any longer. Selena, Hannah, and Matt went up on deck to weigh anchor and get ready to depart. What they saw stopped them in their tracks.

The canal was dotted with floating corpses. Some were dead Infected; some British Army and RAF personnel. Hannah counted at least seven through the driving rain. She pulled the anchor up at the prow, and her trainers slipped under her, and she landed on her behind on the wet deck with a jolt. The anchor splashed back into the water, and she knelt and rubbed at her sore coccyx. Matt seeing this made his way over the roof, nearly falling in himself.

"You okay, you hurt?" he shouted over the rain that filled his mouth, as he helped her to her feet.

"Only my pride," Hannah muttered, feeling confused to be in his arms again.

"Eh?" Matt shouted over the rain and the muffling effect of having his coat hood over his head.

"I said I'm fine," Hannah opted for an easier response. "Let's get this anchor up eh."

"I'll get the anchor up, you get below Han," he said, not really hearing her over the storm like conditions.

Hannah smiled at the use of Han, a shortening of her name she once loved to hear him whisper as they made love in the back of his car. Hannah shook her head and went below out of the driving rain. She saw Ayesha hurrying over to help close the door and get her out of her saturated coat. Seeing Ayesha made her banish any thoughts of Matt to the past section of her memory. She knew he was a louse, a coward, and a user, she just had to keep reminding herself of that fact, even when he was doing nice, caring things for her.

"Looks a bit fucking shit out," Ayesha said, helping her tug off her wet coat.

"And slippery as fuck, I fell on my arse," Hannah said, as they hung her dripping coat by the bow doors.

"Well I ain't kissing it better, but I can make you a coffee if you like," Ayesha said with a smile.

"Cool," Hannah said as they went to the galley area.

"This isn't going to help much," Matt shouted over the squally winds and rain right next to Selena.

"No," Selena shouted back as she aimed the narrowboat into the middle of the canal as they rounded a bend. She was glad she had her own leather gloves on, but her hands were already numb underneath.

"You will need lots of help today, you better show me what to do Captain," Matt offered.

"Okay, take the throttle first, to get the feel of it."

Matt rubbed his cold, wet hands and took over the throttle control first. Once he was *au fait* with that, she taught him how to steer. After they had passed under two concrete bridges, Selena left him to it and went below, glad to be out of the rain and offered a warm tea by Ayesha and Hannah. She changed into a winter pullover from her pack and tried to warm up and dry off before she had to go back out there. Lucky for her, Ellie and Brita volunteered to take the tiller for the next hour and give her an extended break.

Even though the narrowboat passed within twenty yards of houses on each side, beyond the line of ever-present trees, the rain and storm made hearing or even seeing much beyond the next bend of the canal near impossible. There could be a government evacuation safety zone or a hundred hungry driven-mad-by-pain Infected nearby, and they would not spot either.

The water levels of the canal rose again, turning any open garden they saw into lakes and marooning houses in the grey veil that fell from the steely heavens. A freezing cold and wet hour passed and even Tony took a turn up on the tiller. Nothing much changed, the trees looked like they were from some swamp or marsh, their roots and trunks encircled by the flood water. Whoever was *up top* saw no signs of life. Only the odd half sunken boat near the banks, but who would be out in this weather anyway?

Selena, who was back on the wet deck again, had no real clue where they were now, but it was a canal, not a road system. Like a railway track, it went up and down, and you could not get lost, just carry on until you reach the end. She was very glad that they had not seen a lock all day. It was treacherous enough trying to stand on the deck, let alone trying to open, close, and navigate a lock. Apart from a dead cow near one bank, Selena saw nothing but the canal, trees, and rain. And that was fine.

Selena saw a flooded out large stately home on the left bank before she went down below for a warm soup lunch. Matt took over as she shook off the rain and sat down to eat and get the feeling back in her fingers. There wasn't much conversation going on around the cabin, as there wasn't much to say or report. Rain, trees, canal, were the order of the day.

Flooded fields gave way to dense waterlogged woodland and still the rain, and gale force winds lashed the *Ramses Two*. Ellie and Brita took the next go at the tiller, shivering next to each other and not saying much, passing through the woods into lakes of flooded farmland. Only the odd remote farm or church spire was seen above the brown waters that swelled deeper every mile they traversed. The towpaths were no longer visible, and Ellie steered by using the tree line as her guide to judge where the middle of the canal was. Visibility and the constant cold driving rain made progress slow and miserable for whoever took the helm. The submerged fields as far as the eye could see were a wonder to look upon, but depressing also, as there was no chance of rescue for miles on end. No hope of a warm hotel bed again or a home comfort, just an endless flooded inland sea that covered most of this part of Hampshire.

"Look," Brita shouted and pointed to the right bank.

Ellie took a bearing of where she was heading and only then took a peek to where her girlfriend was pointing. The ruins of an ancient worn down castle swept past. It was the most interesting thing they had seen all day. It was soon lost around a bend in the water course and replaced with trees and flood waters again.

Selena knew it was near her turn to go up top again because she had nearly dried out. She looked around the cabin to see Ayesha and Hannah sitting wedged up on the armchair talking in friendly whispers. Then the pale light from the small high windows went ominously dark, one by one and throwing the cabin area into near night-time darkness.

"What the fucks going on?" Tony bellowed from the galley.

Selena rushed aft to grab her coat and open the bow doors. Tony, Ann, and Matt were behind her. Apart from a little dripping water, the darkness above was dry and stank of pond weed.

"Careful, careful," a crouching Ellie warned her as she came up.

Selena saw low arched bricks above as the *Ramses Two* scraped under a low roofed bridge. "Keep your heads down, we are passing under a long low bridge," Selena warned as she skipped past everyone to find the canal map on the table. She turned on the electric lights run off the engines, needing to see where they were. At first, she thought they had somehow gone the wrong way, but then saw her error. Where the blue canal ended, she had wrongly assumed was the dead-end of the canal, what it actually was, was a long tunnel under the

countryside to join up with another blue line on the other fold
of the map. The canal did not end where she had first thought.

Brita switched on the bow lights as they passed through the
tunnel. Yet the boat was so high in the water that the clearance
above the roof was barely two inches in places. Ellie dropped to
a low speed and tried to steer looking back the way they came
to get a reference to the sides of the tight bridge. It did not help,
and they bumped along from side-to-side in the narrow tunnel
and hoped they would not get stuck.

Selena hurriedly scanned the map as Hannah, seeing what
was going on rushed to open the bow doors and see where they
were going. All she saw from the front lamp was darkness and
slimy bricks ahead in the algae green waters. It was like they
were passing from life into the dark abyss of hell and there was
no round exit light in sight.

CHAPTER TWENTY

THE MILL

There was a loud splash, followed in quick succession by another, causing water to spray up in the darkness over Hannah. She didn't know what was happening until the first brick hit the side of the narrowboat and bounced off into the darkness with a splash. The tunnel was coming down on her head. Another brick fell crushing the little finger of her left hand. Hannah pulled it to her mouth and sucked, tasting her own blood.

More and more bricks fell down around her and on her back, knocking her to the floor. The extra weight of the caving in tunnel was pushing the bow under the dark waters of the canal. She tried to rise, but another half brick hit her on the back of the head forcing her down into the cold infection filled waters.

Filling her mouth, with its oily taste.

So she could not catch her breath.

Hannah sat bolt upright in bed, gasping for breath from the drowning nightmare she had woken up from. She caught her breath at last as she rubbed between her breasts in a vain effort to get her body working again. She panted, over and over until she calmed down, but panic took over. The bed? the dark room, where the hell was she?

"Not on the boat, not drowning," she muttered to herself as she pulled the blankets and duvet over the t-shirt she wore to bed. Then like the sluice gate of the many locks they had passed through, it all flooded back to her in an instant.

The mill.

They had been at the mill nearly a week, marooned by the floodwaters. After scraping through the long tunnel, they had followed the canal as far as it could go. The land was mainly farmland, low, flat and under five feet of water. With no suitable dry land left around they had headed off-canal in the narrowboat across the flooded fields, over fences and hedges. Heading south for the coast. It seemed the sensible course of action, not that they had many choices. They had made good ground or water? Then the engine died, fuel gone. The cans they brought with them did not seem to be compatible with the engine fuel, and it coughed a little but did not start. So they drifted across ponds, lakes and swollen fields, helpless to escape.

The rain still beating down and the gale force winds sent them in any possible direction. A grey, wet day turned into an even stormier night. They battened down the hatches and took turns throwing up in the cramped toilet or buckets. Nobody except maybe Tony got any sleep until in the darkest hour of the night they hit something hard and stopped with a scream of the hull dragging across something. She remembered the narrowboat tilting left and then settling. The storm blew itself out, and the rains died. They stumbled seasick and afraid onto the decks to see that they wedged on a low roof between a stone walled shed and the ground floor of a large mill. The side of the mill sloped up at a mad angle to a three-story building. The ground floor was underwater, but the first and third floors were habitable. They secured the *Ramses Two* as best they could and put a plank across from the boat to a window stuck in the middle of the sloped roof.

Apart from the damp cold and the smell wafting up the stairs from the ground floor, it was empty and in good condition. It had been renovated recently and upgraded, but still keeping its original old quirky three-hundred-year-old charm. They transferred their stores from the narrowboat to the mill and settled in.

That had been five days ago. They waited for rescue, but none came. They began to ration meals and water just in case and waited for either the rain to come again and flood them out,

or the waters to abate. There had been the odd spot or spell of
rain, but mostly it was cold and dry out. Slowly the waters began
to recede down the stairs, and the secured narrowboat slid from
its wedged position on long ropes and they moored it next to
the house. They could do nothing but wait and hope for the
flood waters to recede and show them what landscape was left
behind. Behind them to the North was still an endless collection
of lakes. South, they could see hills and green land, probably
the South Downs Matt had informed them. Even when the flood
waters had gone, the ground would be a muddy marsh for days.

"Matt," Hannah whispered and patted the double bed next
to her. It was empty.

She had let him into her bed two nights ago, giving him the
benefit of parental doubt. Sex was out of the question, she had
informed him, snuggling okay if she was in the mood, but no
kissing or caressing. He had been trying really hard since they
became stuck at the mill, and sometimes she needed someone
to hold her close when the waves of grief hit her. He had been a
proper gent the first night. Last night he had groped her breasts
but claimed it was a sleepy accident. Tonight he had crossed the
line; his erection pressing into her lower back. She slapped him
away, and he promised to be good from now on like he was of
school age and not her.

She felt sorry for him, a little, but she wasn't sure what she
wanted from him yet, and sex was not on the cards. That had got
them into this situation in the first place. Hannah giggled, thinking he had probably wandered off to masturbate somewhere.
She lay down, but her mind was whirring from the nightmare,
and thoughts of her family kept flashing into her brain. She got
out of bed, maybe he would be satisfied with her tossing him off
or something. She pulled on her jeans and left the heavy door of
her bedroom.

The mill was huge and had more than enough bedrooms
for the entire group. Brita and Ellie and the Gables had a double
bed each, while Selena, Ayesha, and Matt had singles. The house
was dark and the old boards creaked as her bare feet walked
along them. She checked the main bathroom, but it was dark
and empty. Hannah checked his old room, but he wasn't there.

Frowning, she was about to go back to bed, as she was getting chilly, when she heard noises from Ayesha's room at the far end of the landing.

Noises that brought the cold from the air around her inside the core of her body. She crept closer on the tips of her toes, the familiar sounds booming loud in her mind as she tried to imagine what else they guttural sounds could be. The door was shut, but there was a keyhole. She peered through but the room was dark, and she could only see vague shadowy movements on the bed.

Ayesha moaned loudly with sexual pleasure. Hannah put her ear to the keyhole, then she felt sick, tears welling in her stupid teenage eyes.

"Don't come inside me, come in my mouth," Ayesha said in a direct breathless slow guttural voice. "I ain't going to be your second baby-momma."

"Shssh, you'll wake the whole house up," Matt whispered back and let out a breathless laugh.

Hannah had heard enough, she hurried back to her room and tossed off her jeans and buried her head in her pillow, cursing her stupid self for thinking he was something special or that he could be any type of man she could trust.

She was still eyes wide open when he returned to bed forty minutes later and got in beside her slowly and lay with his back to hers with a satisfied sigh. Hannah's tears of betrayal turned to ones of rage and secret revenge. She did not sleep again that night.

The slap hit Ayesha with such surprise that it floored her before she knew what was going on. The rest of the group gasped going to either Ayesha aid or to get in-between the teen girls.

"What the fuck?" Ayesha said as Ann helped her from the floor of the empty bedroom that they used for a communal room.

"What's going on here?" Ellie asked in-between them. Tony, Brita, and a nervous looking Matt hung back.

"Why did you hit her?" Selena demanded loudly in Hannah's right ear.

"Because she took something without asking," Hannah

replied coldly, staring into Ayesha's glaring eyes. "If you had asked nicely, you could have had the bastard, but you had to betray our friendship."

"Hey, I ain't apologising for anything, I just needed some cock, and the supply is limited. Not like you were giving him any, anyway."

Tony excused himself loudly with a smirk on his big face and raised his hand. Ann gave him a dig in the ribs, so he put his arm around Matt's shoulder. "You dirty fucker, do I have to keep my Ann a safe distance from you now, as you are going for the whole girly group set, stud?"

Matt ducked under his arm and moved near, but not too near the warring girls. "Look, it was all her Han I swear, she seduced me."

"Are you fucking thirteen," Hannah turned her rage at him now. "You're supposed to be a man, not some horny teen. You made promises to be there for me and our child, but you just can't help yourself, can you. I wasn't giving you sex, but I was trusting you again with my heart. You're a fucking mistake of a pathetic fucking joke of a man. I want nothing to do with you ever again, me or the baby." Hannah rushed from the room and locked herself in the bedroom she was using. She wasn't upset for herself, she left before her anger caused her to lay-into Matt or Ayesha.

She knew that would be no good for the group. But why had she slapped Ayesha and not kicked Matt in the nuts, he so deserved it. Maybe her friendship with Ayesha meant more than that sack-of-shit father of her unborn child. She was angry and confused and hurt. When Selena knocked at her door fifteen minutes later, she let her in and rushed into her embrace. Hannah had no love for her dead mother and Selena had never wanted children, but they clung to each other like they were.

Matt was exiled by the group in Hannah's absence to sleep on the narrowboat. He went without argument. His plans for Hannah, festering inside his dirty mind once more. Ayesha braised it out, in her mind, she had done nothing wrong.

Hannah cornered her on the landing after lunch.

"You ain't gonna slap me again are you?"

"Nope, just talk."

"Look, shit, you weren't married or together were you." Ayesha saw the look on Hannah's face and raised her hands defensively. "But I know I did wrong by fucking him, he wasn't even that good."

"So why did you do it then, why did you ruin our friendship for a quick fuck?"

"I don't fucking know, when I get bored or sad I just want sex, I've always been like it. Major character flaw. But I was stupid to do it, cos I hurt you, and you are a mate, and he's just a fucking man."

"Fucking man indeed." Hannah frowned.

"Oops, bad choice of words," Ayesha giggled.

Hannah, in spite of the rage inside her, grinned back. "So what now?"

"We hug it out, or you can have another free slap, I kinda deserve it for fucking Matt, Jesus my standards have slipped."

"Hug it is," Hannah relented and pulled Ayesha close. The anger seemed to drain away as the two friends held each other tightly.

"Hey, junior rugmuncher's club, I'm free now if you are still after a good seeing to," Tony sarcastically bellowed down the landing to them as he headed to his room.

"In ya fucking dreams," Ayesha shot back.

"Wet dreams yes," Tony chuckled and went into his bedroom smiling broadly at his own wit.

"Perve," Hannah said to the closed door.

"Men eh," Ayesha said, and they went back to Hannah's room to talk some more.

It was pitch black outside. The stars were visible all around as there was no orange glow from cities or towns to spoil the view. The figure moved with quiet purpose until it reached its goal. A sharp knife appeared and began to cut hard and deep until its task was accomplished.

CHAPTER TWENTY-ONE

MAROONED

Ann left the warm corner of the bed Tony's large frame had pushed her into, under protest. The sun was shining so bright through the curtains, making the edges glow with almost heavenly light. The floor boards were damp and cold to her bare feet so she pulled on the thick socks she had lying nearby and shuffled to the window. She wished for hot water to bathe her face, but all they had was a dwindling supply of baby wipes. Water was too precious to waste on washing. With face and pits and other parts dampened while sitting on the bed, she pushed herself up and winced as she approached the bright glare of the window. Tony had picked the largest and best room, with an en-suite, but it faced due east and got the full force of the early morning sun. Not that she was complaining at all. Sun was far preferable to storms and the rain bringing floods.

She stood up, looking down. She had a t-shirt on, but it was loose and if she breathed in she was sure she might have even seen her own bush if it weren't for her big pants. Even those were getting loose. The constant stress, lack of food and more exercise than she had done in ten years were shedding the pounds off her. Even Tony's beer gut was decreasing, she had noticed last night during sex.

Ann skirted the corner of one curtain and lifted it up, hoping it would be less of a shock to her eyes. It wasn't. Instead of getting a view of the water levels and the narrowboat below she got orange glare followed by blue pulsing spots where her vision used to be. She held the curtain open and blinked rapidly, her eyes watering for natural reasons rather than emotional ones for a change. Wiping at her eyes, in turn, she shielded her brow and peered down into the waters below that surrounded the mill. She was sure that the water levels had dropped another foot overnight. Maybe if the sun shone all day, it might even sink lower. The mill was okay as a temporary place to stay, but it was damp and the smells coming up from the ground floor were vile. They were marooned here, for the time being. The water would need to be all gone before they could set out again. The narrowboat was useless to them.

Shame, she thought as she let the curtain drop and padded over intending to use the en-suite. She liked the boat even though it made her feel queasy because it saved her walking. She reached the door of the connected bathroom when it hit her like a thunderbolt. She ran back to the window and pulled the curtains wide open, engulfing the bedroom in warm morning sunshine.

"What the fuck?" Tony moaned from the bed, waking up, his arm over his eyes to protect him from the intense glare.

"The narrowboat."

"What about it," Tony grumbled, swinging his massive legs out of bed. "It ain't sunk, has it gurl?"

"No, it's fucking gone Tone."

"What you mean gone?" Tony stumbled around the wooden frame of the bed, managing to stub his toe, so he ended up limping to the window saying, "Shitshitshit," under his breath.

"It ain't there anymore, look for yourself." Ann pointed out the window to where the *Ramses Two* had been moored. The mooring ropes dangled into the water, but the narrowboat that should be right in front of them was nowhere to be seen. They scanned the flat waterlogged land as far as they could see from their window, but could see no sign of the narrowboat.

"Should we tell the others?" Ann peered about the flooded yard below.

"You think?"

"Where the bloody hell has it gone?" Ellie was the first to vocalise what the rest of the group were thinking.

"Hang on, if the *Ramses Two* has gone, where's Matt?" Hannah pointed out.

The group looked around, Matt had been banished to the narrowboat, now he and the boat were missing.

"He was on the boat last night," Selena said.

"Has he left without us then, cut the ropes and drifted off, leaving us all behind?" Brita addressed the pertinent question of the morning.

"Maybe the moorings came loose or broke," Ayesha added.

"Or maybe you girls pissed him off so much he'd rather float off on his todd, rather than be around you birds all the time, giving him grief." Tony mimed his hand speaking, just to add to his point.

"Maybe you should shut the fuck up," Brita raised her voice.

"Fuck you dyke," Tony took a menacing step towards Brita, but she had brought the automatic rifle with her and aimed it at the big man. "One day you'll leave that somewhere and wake up the next day with it rammed up your snatch."

"Promises, promises," Brita taunted him back.

"Leave it," Ann urged, pulling back on her husband's arm.

"This isn't helping, is it?" Selena stood between them. "The boat is gone, and we are trapped here until the waters recede, so we better ration the food and water some more and try and get along with each other. All this infighting won't help us survive this mess. We've done well so far, by uniting together."

"Have we done so well though?" Ellie piped up.

"What do you mean?" Selena turned to her.

"We are stuck here on the whims of the weather and the Red Death infection. Anyone of us could be struck down at any moment. The food and water is dwindling. We've lost people we've cared about along the way."

"What do you expect us to do, give up?" Selena asked.

"I'm not saying that. I'm saying things might get a whole lot worse before they get better again."

"No offence luv, but as a cheerleader, you kinda suck," Ayesha wiggled her right forefinger at Ellie.

"Hey, stop this. None of this is helping," Brita said, stepping protectively in front of her girlfriend.

"How about we all get dressed, and all take a different window to look out of to see if we can see the *Ramses* anywhere," Hannah said loudly, hands on hips. "How does that sound?"

"Better than listening to all this *Women's Hour* bollocks," Tony said, and everyone trooped out of the Gable's bedroom in single file.

"You okay, Tony?" Ann asked as her husband leant his knuckles into the windowsill and peered outside.

"One day I'm going to sort that foreign dyke bitch out once and for all," he muttered to his faint reflection in the glass panes.

Ann didn't like the edge to his voice as he said it.

"What do you think?" Hannah pulled the end of the mooring rope up out of the water wearing a marigold glove she had found under the sink in the main bathroom cabinet.

"Fucking hell you're asking me. I don't know one end of a piece of rope from another," Ayesha said, staring at the end of the rope.

"Well you won't make a good Doctor Watson, will you?" Hannah peered closer at the severed rope.

"Doctor Who?"

"Nah that's a different programme," Hannah smiled back, but seeing the nonplussed look on her friend's face, she gave up on the geek humour. "Does it look cut through to you?"

"Suppose." Ayesha shrugged. She was bored investigating. The sun was hot on the tiles of the low sloping roof at least.

"So, did Matt cut the ropes to drift off to get away from us, or did someone else cut it to give the same end result?"

"Fucking hell does it matter, the numb nuts is gone and good riddance I say, we can do so much better. Obviously not here at the mill, but after all this shit has gone done, we can go out clubbing together."

"Erm, pregnant girl," Hannah pointed out.

"Oh yeah, forget about that sometimes."

"Wish I could, it's all I think about some days. What kind of world will my child be born into? The old world as it used to be or this soggy infected nightmare."

"It will get sorted won't it, then we can get back to normal again."

"Normal?" Hannah threw the rope back into the water below. "My entire family is gone."

"Mine too, remember, you can stay with me at my place in Surbiton, stick together through thick and thin, shag the same men, all that shit," Ayesha grinned and lightly punched Hannah's arm.

"Let's get off this roof before we slip off it." The two teens helped each other over to the window and clambered back inside. Hannah took one last look around the water covered countryside and wondered where the father of her child was and how had he got there?

It took three days for the flood waters to recede enough for the group to venture down the stairs of the mill. In the end, they wished they hadn't. The flood waters may have gone, but left behind was a foot of muddy, stinking sludge that covered the floor and every surface. Even if there was food in the kitchen, no one was willing to risk searching through it.

The last three days since the narrowboat had vanished had been a slow descent into hell. Lack of food, water and being cramped together didn't help at all. Brita and Ellie locked themselves away, keeping out of the Gables' way as much as possible. Selena was hated because she had been voted to take care of the dwindling supplies and divvy them up. Tony's hunger had turned his mood into dark places. Leaving Ann with bruised ribs and tender behind where he had taken his belt off to her for some wrong word she could not recall. She placated him with sex on tap, which had lost any tenderness. She had become a vessel to funnel his rage so he would not take it out on the other women in the mill. She knew he might hurt her, but he loved her enough not to go too far. With Brita though, Ann feared Tony might just strangle her with his bare hands in one dark rage if he had the chance. Lucky for her she had the rifle and knew how to use it.

Ann always volunteered to fetch the doled-out food and water and gave three-quarters of it to her husband. The only good thing was the dramatic weight loss, but it meant the punches hurt more as she had less meat to protect her. Seeing the yard and the actual river that spun the wheel of the mill had made her smile for the first time in ages. They had to leave soon or end up dead one way or the other.

"Okay we are down to our last meal and the water situation is dire also," Selena stated to the group two days later. "We have no choice now, but to leave the mill and find either another house or shop."

"Then we pack our shit and go," Ayesha said, rubbing at her always hungry stomach. She had once thought feeling your ribs would be a good look, now she knew that was puerile bullshit. She wanted bacon, a Big Mac with fries and a whole lot of wine and cake to wash it down. Skinny wasn't all it was cracked up to be.

"What about the mud and still flooded places?" Ann asked trying not to show the pain caused by her bruised ribs.

"We have no choice but to go. We'll try to find a road that maybe isn't under the water and hope for the best," Selena answered her.

"Let's just fucking eat and then go," Tony almost grunted out his words.

"Then we are all agreed, eat drink and then find someplace else?" Hannah said.

They were all too eager to eat, but everyone acknowledged that staying at the farm would kill them all. One way or the other.

They left after ten. The sky was blue with patchy clouds that ran swiftly across the heavens under the steam of a strong buffeting wind. They wrapped up warm and took what water and cans of drink they had left. The landscape was flat leading up to the downs ahead. Green lush grass, fields of brown mud and pools of water from pond to lake size were dotted around the surrounding countryside. The farmland was crisscrossed with hedges and lines of trees making their field of vision limited from the ground.

It was hard going because of the sucking mud in places. They had to skirt large still flooded dips and swollen streams, and it took them an hour to reach a road. They had passed two cottages without noticing because of the high hedges and dips in the ground they trudged through.

The single lane country road crossed their path, so they headed left until they found a road off it leading south towards the high ground and the way they wanted to go. The muddy but firm road became tight and enclosed by overhanging trees covered with dark green ivy. They walked along, glad of a firm footing underfoot, unable to see anything but the road ahead. Then out of the hedgerows, five very different styled houses appeared to their left and right through broken wooden gates. The most pretty being a thatched cottage, with the muddy remains of a once pretty 'chocolate box' cottage garden. Three were bungalows from the sixties and seventies and the last a two-storey converted barn.

"Which one should we try first?" Ellie said staring at the flood water marks up the side of the cottage.

"Let's split up into three groups and search that way, cos I'm fucking half starved," Tony suggested, grabbing Ann's hand and heading for the first bungalow on the left.

Much as she hated to agree with the Neanderthal, Selena could see the logic in his thinking.

"Come on," Ellie urged Brita as they headed through the gate, stuck half ajar by mud, towards the cottage.

Hannah and Ayesha made for the next bungalow to the right, leaving Selena alone on the road. "Come on slow coach," Hannah turned and called back to her. Smiling, Selena followed after the two teens. Somebody had to keep them out of trouble, now that they were both orphans.

The cottage was a complete right off, and they could see nothing to drink or eat that wasn't covered with the slime and mud of the flood waters. The bungalows were the same, the flood waters had passed through and submerged them, tainting everything in its path. The group met up outside the barn, it too had suffered because of the flood waters. They could see the water levels had risen to over five feet on the magnolia painted walls. The kitchen and the whole ground floor was a broken mess. Furniture, televisions, table and chairs had been swept into a corner by the sheer force of the rising waters. Ayesha, Selena, and Hannah went upstairs with little hope but came down with a few prizes. Two half full bottles of water on each nightstand of the master bedroom. Three bottles of champagne next to a corkboard filled with horse riding rosettes and show jumping awards and pictures. Plus, half a packet of stale, but still edible digestives.

Tony took one bottle of champagne to share with Ann, even though the others warned him not to drink on an empty stomach. The others drank the remains of one of the bottles of water between them. Saving the heavy bottles of champagne as a last resort. They had had two digestives each, the spare they gave to Hannah as she was eating for two. They rested in the upstairs for half an hour, used the facilities and then had to press on.

They walked on down the road, finding the next two homes and a kennels had been partially knocked down in places. The kennels had been flattened like a tornado had hit it. The sight of five or so dogs lying in pools of stagnant water and mud was heart-breaking. Even Tony winced at the sight of the drowned animals.

They hurried on as quickly as they could manage.

A mile further on down the road they passed some more bungalows, but these were still underwater. Through the broken front door of the other bungalow, they could see the bare and withered foot and leg of a child sticking out of a wave of sludge and water. The group tried not to rubber-neck and moved on around the bend.

The road ran down ending at a road bridge across a waterlogged set of railway tracks. Wedged across the road and stuck in hedges and trees on either side was the *Ramses Two*.

CHAPTER TWENTY-TWO

STILL WATERS RUN DEEP

"Fuck me old boots!" Tony blew out his cheeks as the group rounded his huge frame to get a better look at their old floating home.

"Matt?" Ellie called up at the slightly tipped narrowboat, knowing most of the people there wouldn't bother. The narrowboat had a hole in the bow where it had wedged into a tree trunk, but apart from that, it looked sound.

No answer came from the narrowboat.

Brita hurried forwards and scrambled nimbly up the tree to gain access to the boat and went below as the others waited outside. Brita appeared at the other end of the boat a long minute later: alone. "He's not here nor his stuff. There is some water left in the tank so we can refill our bottles at least and I found a tin of beans in the cupboard." Brita held the blue bean tin aloft like it was a winning trophy.

Brita filled all the water bottles they had and then passed down mugs of water for them to drink their fill until the tank ran dry and the taps just dripped. She cooked up the beans on the gas stove onboard, and everyone at least had two hot mouthfuls each. Then they had to decide what to do next. The road ran down into a vast flooded flat stretch of land, so they left the road and headed east along the top of the embankment above the submerged railway tracks. They could see the roofs of a town below in the small valley, flooded up to the gutters so there was no use trying to go there.

The railway embankment rose, leaving it as the only piece

of dry land for miles. They followed its course having no alternatives. Walking along the tracks again, surrounded by glistening water took them back.

"Like old times," Ann said to Tony as they lagged behind the others.

"Shit walking on railway tracks, old times yeah," he grunted, ending that conversation.

After a mile, they came to a road that passed over the railway tracks and gave them a little hope. The road was higher than others they had seen so they headed down it as they could see large buildings, bungalows and a farm ahead through the hedges. The bungalows were washed out messes, but a huge farm with tall, long sheds on a road to the left held more promise. It was on the crest of an incline and looked like it had escaped the worst of the flooding. There were signs of a village below, but this was near a stream and most of it looked still underwater in places.

"Farm?" Selena suggested.

Everyone was weary so agreed.

Brita and Ellie took the lead. They passed a tall wooden structure to their right and a large tree on a rise to their left. Across the road were swung two iron cattle gates, with a red tractor parked in the middle. The gates were chained to it to prevent any vehicles from coming up the road.

Hannah glanced at a small field to the left past the tree, it was empty of animals, and she wondered if it was a cattle or cereal farm. A motherly protective feeling of danger and unease ran through Hannah's body as she stopped dead on the farm road. Ayesha noticed she had stopped and turned to face her friend. Piers' axe wrapped up over her left shoulder. "You okay?"

"I dunno, I've got a weird feeling all of a sudden."

"What sort of weird feeling?" Ayesha asked with a quick glance at the group. Ellie and Brita were approaching the gates, with the others a few steps behind.

"I'm super scared for some reason, and I don't know why."

"Weird," Ayesha commented.

Brita and Ellie had reached the gate and parted to look around the tractor, which was blocking their view. Brita who had gone left looked past the tractor at the farm buildings beyond and readied her rifle. Ellie could not see much so she clambered onto the first two rungs of the five-bar gate. It rattled a little, making a noise, but was secure.

"What's that?" Selena had come up to the side of Brita and pointed to something swinging in the second tree along, which was overhanging the road.

"I think I can see someone, hey?" Ellie called from the other side of the tractor.

"Oh no?" Brita looked as the thing on the tree swung round to reveal a man's body hung by the neck from the tree with a white sign around his neck. He looked like he had been pecked at by carrion. The sign simply read: NO TRESPASSERS! "Ellie get down!" Brita shouted and ran towards her girlfriend.

"Eh?" Ellie turned to face Brita before half of her face exploded sending blood, bones and one eye flying everywhere. Ellie fell from the gate onto the hard wet road dead.

"Run," Ayesha urged dragging Hannah back down the road they came. Another shotgun blast from behind the wooden structure felled them both.

"Noooooo," Brita raised the automatic rifle and put one shot through the right eye of the farmer holding the double-barrel shotgun, killing him outright. Shots exploded off the side of the tractor, smashing two of the windows. Brita ducked, only hit by falling glass. She raised the rifle again and put two rounds into the chest of a younger man firing from behind a tree to the left. He fell screaming, but his cries for help soon gurgled into nothing.

Seeing no immediate threat, Brita dropped to her knees next to Ellie.

There was no life left in the ruins of her face. Her one remaining eye stared up at the sky. Brita pulled Ellie up onto her knees, feeling the dead weight of her body. She hugged the ruined side of her face into her core and let out a wail of loss. Around her people screamed, ran, shouted, and cried out in pain, but she took none of it in. Brita's world, her capacity to love and her belief that *this time* there may be a happy ending, died on that farm road with Ellie.

Selena rushed over to the two teens, scared to her wits about them. Both lay still, with bloody wounds on their backs and shoulders. Ann lay prone on the road, hands over her ringing ears screeching like a banshee.

Ayesha sat up with a roar of pain, grabbing for her axe.

Tony, roaring like a tank crashed through the wooden fence without stopping and kicked the head of the former farmer like a football in his rage. It snapped like a twig. He picked up the shotgun, ejected the cartridges and fished in the pockets of the farmer's green waxed jacket for more. He found five cartridges and loaded two, then charged over to the nearby farmhouse to see if there were anymore shotgun happy locals to exact his revenge. Tony might not have liked Brita, but Ellie was a pretty harmless part of his group. Nobody attacked him and got away with it.

"Is she okay?" Ayesha said, jumping to her feet, a feral rage blazing in her eyes.

"I think so," Selena turned Hannah over, there was a cut on her forehead when she hit the road, and it was bruising fast. The young schoolgirl gave a groan, and her eyes fluttered open. That was enough for Ayesha. "Stay with her."

"Where are you going, you're bleeding," Selena called after her as Ayesha ran after Tony, heading for the farmhouse.

Ayesha didn't answer, she was full of grief, and rage at the deaths of ones she loved. She ran through the hole in the fence Tony had made with only a glance at poor Brita, cradling her dead love to her middle. Her wails of woe and Ann's cries of hyperventilating fear spurred her on to run faster. She felt no pain, only a cold, wet feeling on her shoulders and back.

Tony just reached the farmhouse door before her, and he kicked it in, breaking the lock through the wooden door-frame. It juddered in, and the two raging group members ran into the house intent on revenge. A short hallway lined with dirty wellingtons led through to a large kitchen. A young lad of Hannah's age with rosy red cheeks was holding a shotgun. He and a heavy-set woman holding a bloody stained chopper looked at them both with utter surprise.

The lad levelled the shotgun at Tony, but the big man fired

first, discharging both barrels by accident, as he was not used to handling shotguns. The first shot blew off the kid's hands and the almost immediate second shot turned his stomach into a collider of bloody flesh. The lad went down screaming, looking at the diced mess that had been his hands. He slumped against a kitchen cabinet, as Tony broke the barrel to reload.

"Eddy," the woman brandishing the meat cleaver cried out and then her face turned into a snarl, and she ran at Tony. He raised the shotgun to protect himself, but he hadn't even got the spent cartridges out yet.

Piers' fireman's axe embedded deep into the woman's skull stopping her in her tracks. She staggered, dropped the cleaver and turned to look at the raging face of Ayesha. She opened her mouth to say something, but no words came out, and she collapsed to the kitchen flagstones dead.

"Mum," the boy cried out in loss and pain, raising a stump towards her.

"Enough of this shit," Tony snarled, grabbing a carving knife from the kitchen table, he thrust it deep into the boy's left eye, killing him instantly. Calmly, Tony put new cartridges into the shotgun and then grabbed the boy's bloody weapon from the floor. The stock was a little splintered, but it looked in working order still. He thrust it into Ayesha's hands.

"Let's make sure there are no more of these sheep shagging cunts about."

Ayesha nodded.

They moved through the house. Tony pointed for her to search downstairs while he checked the upstairs rooms. She nodded again and moved through the house, adrenaline coursing through her fired up veins. She almost ran through the rooms, daring for someone to attack her so she could end their life in the most painful way ever. There was a woman's scream from upstairs and then the sound of a struggle, a short cry and then nothing.

Ayesha continued her search. The downstairs was empty of anyone else. She headed for the stairs, breathing hard, and feeling the aching pain in her shoulder at last. The aching became a proper eye-stinging pain, and she gritted her teeth as a wave of nausea flowed up from her belly. She went into a tiny toilet and threw up. When she came out, Tony was dragging a woman in her twenties down the stairs by the back of her collar. She had long black hair, and a nasty gash above her cocked-askew glasses.

"Anybody else?"

"No," Ayesha wiped her mouth as she shook her head, "place is clear now."

"You look like shit, and you're bleeding."

"I feel shaky as shit, man."

"Sit down in the living room, I'll tie this bitch up and go fetch the others." Tony pulled the woman to her feet by the hair, causing her to howl. "Shut the fuck up." He dragged her by the hair into the kitchen. Ayesha heard the woman scream with grief and begin to sob as she saw the bloody mess of the mother and son. She was probably a relative too.

"Sit still," she heard Tony shout, followed by a hard slap of hand to bare skin. Ayesha winced at the sound, glad it wasn't her. She put down the shotgun and tried to pull her jacket off, the pain and the light-headedness she felt caused her to black out.

When she came to, she was face down in a twin bed. Just across from her in a light, airy bedroom was Hannah. She was topless and laying front down like her. At first, her foggy brain thought they were at some spa weekend, but as she sat up, she winced in pain and saw that Selena was sitting down on Hannah's bed with bandages in her hands.

Ayesha looked down to see her bra was off, and she had a men's loose t-shirt on she did not recognise. Something pulled at her skin, and she winced in pain as she sat up. Her wounds had been dressed while she had been unconscious.

"She okay?"

"I am here you know," Hannah smiled through the pain. "don't get shot of me that easy. Shot, get it?"

"Yes, but it ain't funny," Ayesha smiled, glad she wasn't too badly wounded, it seemed. The fresh bandages on Hannah's back were a little stained with blood, but nothing too bad looking. "Am I okay?"

"You are both okay," Selena replied as she tied off and taped down Hannah's shotgun pellet wounds. "I've got all the shot out, lucky for you both you weren't close and didn't get the full force of the blast."

"How's everyone else, how's Brita?" Ayesha said crossing her legs on the bed.

A troubled look crossed Selena's face. "She's still out there, won't let anyone touch Ellie's body or help her move her. Everyone else is inside, Ann is a bag of nerves but unhurt. But we have other worries."

"Let me guess Tony and that woman he caught?"

"He's treating her like a prisoner of war. He's got her tied to a chair right in front of her dead brother and mother-in-law sobbing her heart out, poor thing."

"Her family killed Ellie and shot me and Hannah, too right she should be tied up." Ayesha put her feet on the floor and stood up. The pain in her shoulder aided her views on the woman they captured.

"This isn't a war you know, Ayesha. She has lost her husband and family today, killed by a bunch of strangers. How would you feel?" Selena said, trying to get some compassion back into the teenage woman.

"I've already lost everyone I've ever loved. Save your pity for Brita and me and Hannah there." Ayesha was angry and left Hannah and Selena in the bedroom and went downstairs.

"You can see I'm right, Hannah, can't you, violence just begets violence."

"Normally I would say you are right, but for now, the world isn't normal. It is a war every day for us just to survive. All the time our group gets less and less. Unless we fight back, we will all die."

Selena went to speak and then pressed her lips tight together. She had no moral high ground to preach from anymore. She wasn't a judge and Hannah not a schoolgirl or the others what jobs or family roles that used to define them. They were gone for the time being. Selena just hoped at the end of this they could all find a way back to a normal civilised life.

Ayesha wiggled her left arm in its socket as her wound itched and she was scared to scratch it and make it bleed again. She walked past the living room. Ann was sitting in the very armchair that she had passed out on, drinking gin straight from the bottle. She looked haggard and rattled. Ayesha didn't blame her, having someone shooting at you for no good reason was terrifying. They weren't soldiers, used to combat situations, yet they had to learn and adapt fast to the situation that they were now in.

In the kitchen, Tony stood leant against the table, a beer to his lips.

"Got any more of those?" Ayesha asked.

"Through there," Tony nodded to a grey painted door next to the large oven. The woman Tony had captured was tied to a wooden chair. Her broken glasses on the floor, her lips and nose stained with dry blood. Ayesha winced seeing her face, but then thought of Ellie's face being blown off, and her feeling of revulsion went away. She walked around the dead bodies of the mother and son and through the grey door into a pantry area. The place had shelves stocked full of food and beverages. She picked a cool bottle of beer from the plastic remains of a six-pack and headed back into the kitchen. She wished she had brought her trainers down with her, as there was so much blood spilt on the flagstones.

Tony picked up something metal from the table and tossed it to her. She caught it in her free hand: it was a bottle opener. Ayesha popped the top and took a long swig. It felt good to drink alcohol again, and it eased her dry throat. "Shouldn't we move the bodies outside?"

This brought a whimper from the woman captive.

"Yeah, they do make the place looks kind of messy don't they. I'll do it once I've had me beer."

"Murderers," the tied up woman hissed.

Tony tipped his beer up and finished it off. Then he smashed the bottle against the table leaving the neck and a jagged end. Ayesha jumped. The poor woman wet herself. Tony bent down and held a long sharp edge of the bottle against and then inside one of the woman's bloody nostrils. "Takes one to know one eh."

"What about Brita and poor Ellie?" Ayesha was getting scared and tried to change the subject.

"Ellie was one of us until your mates blew her pretty fucking head off." Tony flicked the bottle sideward cutting a rent in the woman's nose and causing her to cry out in pain. "But we soon killed them both."

"Please no, not Nathan," the woman wailed as blood dripped onto her blouse, next to her tears.

"It's okay, he only suffered for a little while. Wonder if he thought of you when he drew his last earthly?" Tony sneered into her face.

She tried to head butt him, but Tony reared back with that booming laugh of his.

"You fucking bastards we were only trying to defend our land. The village was drowned, and all these bloody monster things attacked us, then people came, and we tried to help them, but they were only after our food, weapons, and other things." She shouted through her pain and grief.

"Ah boo-hoo, family dead, hubby dead, maybe I should stick this bottle where the sun don't shine and give you a bit of a thrill eh."

Ayesha felt cold again. Tony's behaviour was crossing a line, and she was getting scared. Luckily, Ann, Selena, and Hannah turned up in the kitchen.

"What are you doing to that girl?" Ann asked her husband.

"Just fucking about." Tony stood up and tossed the remains of the bottle in the sink with a smash.

"Looks like you were torturing her to me," Selena said, looking less than amused.

"Fucking deserves it."

"Does she? Has she ever done anything to us personally?" Selena continued.

"Oh don't fucking get on ya moral high horse. I'm gonna take the *stiffs* outside." He grabbed the young lad by the boots and dragged him to the back door, leaving a trail of blood behind. The sight of her brother-in-law being pulled from the kitchen made the woman whimper even more.

"Someone should check on Brita," Ayesha suggested, staring straight at Hannah.

"If you want," Hannah said moving around the blood-stained body of the farmer's wife. She was glad to get away from the blood and carnage. She had seen enough death and blood for one day. She skirted the red dragging lines to the open back door of the farmhouse. She looked back and was unlucky enough to see Ayesha step on the dead woman's head and wiggle the axe from her skull.

Hannah hurried around the corner of the house and threw up over a small hedge.

"Better get used to more of that soon," Tony called to her as he returned from a nearby wooden barn, brushing at his dirty hands.

Before she could reply, Hannah heaved up again as her stomach cramped up. Tony made another snide comment as he re-entered the house, but she didn't catch it over the sounds of her own retching. Tears filled her eyes and for once she was glad of the cold weather, to cool her down. A breeze got up as she crossed the path up to the hole in the fence. Hugging her arms around her middle she stopped, seeing that Brita had not moved from her kneeling position, Ellie's ruined pale face cradled to her blood-stained stomach.

Hannah had to close her eyes again and try not to be sick. She wiped away her renewed tears and breathed slowly.

"Why?"

The strained question forced Hannah to open her eyes. Brita was looking up at her, her tear stained face pleading for answers that Hannah could not give. She had asked them so many times since her grandparents and sister had died. Even before that, at an early age, when her psychotic drug crazed mother had killed her father, stabbed Hannah and then killed herself. *Why?*

"I dunno," Hannah managed to croak.

"She was kind and beautiful and had so much love to give, why not me. I'd swap places with her in an instant." Brita cried out while holding Ellie's cold body to hers as if to give some of her warmth to her lover's corpse.

"I know you would," Hannah said kindly, moving a few steps closer.

"I want to join her, be with her forever."

"Nooo," Hannah cried out a little too slow on the uptake. She rushed forwards as Brita grabbed the automatic rifle, jammed it into her mouth and pulled the trigger.

CHAPTER TWENTY-THREE

THE FARMHOUSE

"So what shall we do with this one then?" Ayesha had asked as Tony walked back into the kitchen after dragging out the dead farmer's wife.

"Put her out of her fucking misery," Tony said, matter-of-factly, as he went over to wash his hands under the cold tap in the sink.

"Don't you dare," Selena stepped forwards, forcing Ayesha with her blood-covered axe to retreat a step. "She did not kill Ellie or shoot at us, we should just let her go."

"What if she comes back with more cousins and more shotguns and kills Hannah or Ann or you?" Ayesha wasn't giving up on her hard line stance, even if it meant siding with Tony.

"Good point," Tony sniffed drying his hands on a nearby dishcloth.

"I've not done anything to you, but you've killed my Nathan and his family," the woman said through her blood and snot covered lips.

"We could make her clean this place up for a start," Ann suggested. She hated that Ellie was dead, but this woman had not pulled the trigger.

"Maybe," Ayesha said lowering her axe.

"Where are the cleaning things around here? Mops and brushes and the like?" Selena asked, eager to follow a less aggressive route.

"End of the pantry through the end door is all the mops, brooms, and buckets. I've done nothing to you, just untie me and leave me alone to mourn for my husband, please, I won't be any trouble I promise. I've never hurt anyone in my life." The woman began to sob again.

"We ain't going anywhere luv, this farm belongs to us now for the foreseeable future. Call it, the spoils of war." Tony sneered at the bound sobbing woman, as he leant back against the sink.

"But this is my home, it's been in my husband's family for eight generations."

"And it would have been for nine, if you hadn't fired at us, injured me and my friend and killed Ellie, she's lying out on the road with half her face blown off." Ayesha leered into the woman's face with rising anger.

"This isn't helping anything, Ayesha, go fetch the mops and buckets. She can help clean this place up while we figure out what to do with her. How does that sound," Ann butted in, trying to stop any more blood being spilled. She could see what it had done to Tony. All the death had affected Ayesha; turning her from a ditsy party girl into a cold-blooded axe-murderer. "I'll come with you."

"Go on Ayesha," Selena urged.

"Don't you think this is over, sister." Ayesha jabbed a finger at the woman. Reluctantly she followed Ann through the pantry door and along until they reached two further doors, one directly ahead and one to the right. The right-hand handle was nearest so she tried that. The door was locked, but a big key with a frayed string attached was looped over a nail on a nearby wall. Intrigued, Ayesha unlocked the door and pushed it open. She was surprised to find a set of stone steps leading down into the darkness of a cellar and a light switch on the grey flaky painted wall. She switched it on, but it brought no illumination, only a strangled cry of sobbing fear from below. Ayesha exchanged a bemused look with Ann, who stood next to the other door.

"Please don't hurt me again," a shaky male voice called up from somewhere below. Gripping the axe, Ayesha hurried down the stone steps to find the source of the frightened voice.

The automatic rifle clicked empty, and Brita threw it away in disgust. It skidded under the tractor. Wailing with grief, she bent over Ellie and hugged even tighter, not wanting to let go.

"Brita, please," Hannah said breathing hard, her heart racing.

Brita just rocked back and forth with Ellie in her arms.

"Let's take her inside eh, find a place for her to rest and then find a nice dry place to bury her." Hannah reached out and touched the grieving woman's shoulder.

Brita flinched away and scrambled back on her behind a metre. "Don't touch us."

"You have to let her go, let her lie in peace, Brita please."

"I don't want to let her go, not ever, you hear," Brita shouted back.

"She's gone."

"No," Brita shook her head.

"She wouldn't want you to kill yourself or give up, she believed in the group, and we are here for you, as you two were here for all of us. Bring her inside and then I'll help you dig a grave on the hillside maybe. It's cold out here, is Ellie warm?"

"She's cold," she admitted squeezing Ellie's lifeless hand.

"Then bring her inside," Hannah said, tears rolling down her cheeks.

"She needs warming up," Brita said, clambering to her feet while holding Ellie's limp body in her arms.

Hannah went to help, but Brita sniffed up her tears. "I can hold her."

Hannah followed behind as Brita carried Ellie's body down to the back door of the farmhouse. She never felt as proud and as sad for someone else in her short life. She followed Brita down the path and into the farmhouse. Tony, Selena and even the woman tied to the chair bowed their heads as Brita walked through the kitchen. Hannah raced past and led her upstairs to find a bed to lay Ellie in and wrap a cover over her.

"We should go back and fetch my Tony," Ann whispered onto Ayesha's shoulder as they crept down the bending stone steps into the cellar. She turned on a torch she had found dangling from a nail just inside the doorway.

"You're safe with me," Ayesha replied coldly, raising the axe as they went down the stairs. They could hear the painful whimpers of a man from round the bend.

They turned a bend and stepped down into a cellar. It was full of junk, a fridge freezer, a washing machine and boxes of family things. At the far end of the cellar was a large metal workbench that was bolted to the floor. Tied to one table leg, sitting in a puddle of his own piss, with his hands tied over his head to a ring on the bench was Matt.

He was stripped to his jeans and t-shirt, and both were ripped and had blood stains on them. His left eye was yellow and black and puffed up so his eye was a slit. His lips looked like they had both been split and there was blood on his arms and wrists.

"Matt?" Ann called over to the cowering man.

Hearing his name, he looked up at them with his one good eye. "Ann, Ayesha?"

"Shit, what have these fuckers done to you?" Ayesha said as the two women raced over to help him.

"Get me free, please, before they come back," he said in a meek voice.

"They won't be coming back, we put paid to that," Ayesha said bending down to untie his legs, trying not to let the smell of his stale piss bother her.

Ann found a sharp knife on the work bench and leant over Matt to cut his hands free. She stopped, the knife held above his bonds. "Oh fuck."

"What?" Ayesha said, freeing his legs and standing up. Below them, Matt began to weep loudly. She was about to say *what* again when she saw what they had done to him. The little finger and ring finger of his left hand were missing. Yet not missing, they sat in the upturned bowl of a clay pigeon. Just behind his bound hands. Ayesha spent no time in cutting him free.

"What happened to you?" Ann asked as they helped their pale companion to his feet.

"They captured me two days ago, with two other men I fell in with after the narrowboat had been set adrift. We came up here to find some food. They shot the others dead and then knocked me out and locked me down here. Some bloody woman kept coming down asking questions and then when she didn't like the answers tortured me and cut off my fingers. They are all fucking mad the lot of them, but the other woman was the worst, she never asked questions, just liked inflicting pain on me. I've never done anything to them at all." Matt sobbed.

Ann and Ayesha took an arm each and carried him from his prison.

"You're safe now," Ann assured him.

"You sure?"

"Yes. Cos we bloody killed most of them," Ayesha said as they helped him from the cellar.

"You going to be okay?" Hannah asked as Brita laid Ellie on the single bed and pulled a sheet up over her ruined face. It soon was stained crimson with blood.

"We just need to be left alone," Brita mumbled.

"As long as you promise not to do anything stupid, we need you, Brita."

Brita pulled the curtains to shut out the day and lay on the bed next to her beloved Ellie. Hannah stood for a second, not knowing what to do for the best. In the end, all she could do was retreat from the room and hope that Brita did not find another way to kill herself. She was heading downstairs when she heard shouts and commotion from the kitchen. She ran in. To her total astonishment, she found a pale, bloodied Matt stabbing the bound woman in the chest over and over again with a carving knife, as the others tried to hold him back.

Hannah stopped at the door, mouth agape, until she remembered to breathe. The carving knife got stuck in the dead woman's ribcage and finally Tony was able to wrestle him back from his mad melee attack. Only with his hands held up as Tony held his wriggling body, did Hannah see Matt's mutilated left hand.

"What the hell is going on here?" Hannah cried out.

Matt, crying and shaking with rage, turned in Ayesha and Tony's arms to see her at the doorway. "Han?"

"Matt, what happened to you?" Hannah tip-toed around the pools of blood on the kitchen floor, just in time to see Matt faint dead away in Tony's arms.

"Ann and I found him tied up in the cellar, he said they had been torturing him and a woman cut off his fingers, the fucking bastards," Ayesha explained.

"I guess we know which one cut his fingers off then?" Ann pointed at the dead woman with a kitchen knife protruding out of her chest.

"I don't understand; how did he get here?"

"Dunno Han, Let's get him to a bed eh," Ayesha said, as Tony let the two teens struggle with the unconscious Matt. They put an arm around each of their necks and half carried and half dragged him out of the kitchen. His socks leaving tram lines on the blood-splattered floor.

"I'll get this one outside with the others." Tony just grabbed the backrest of the chair and dragged the dead woman, still bound to it, outside.

"Let's get this place cleaned up," Ann said clapping her hands together and staring at Selena, the only one of their group left in the kitchen.

"Yeah," Selena nodded and followed Ann into the pantry and the walk-in cupboard with mops and bottles of cleaning liquids.

Hannah and Ayesha took Matt into the living room and laid him on the sofa. They couldn't have managed to get him upstairs anyway. Their shoulders hurt from their minor shot-gun wounds. He had lost a few pounds since this nightmare had all begun, but he was still an eleven stone deadweight.

Ayesha hurried off upstairs to the bathroom to find a green medicine box she had spotted earlier while having a pee. Hannah pushed another cushion under Matt's head and made him comfortable as she could. He looked pale, dirty and his face had taken a few punches since she had seen him last. His left hand was covered in crusted red and brown blood. She gently raised it up onto his chest and kept her hand there just to make sure his heart was still beating. It was, and she could see his chest rise and fall slightly. His breathing through his bloodied nose whistled slightly.

Ayesha reappeared carrying a green medicine box in one

hand. A plastic jug filled with water and cotton wool balls in the other. She knelt down next to Hannah and set them both on a coffee table next to the end of the sofa.

Hannah stared at the jug of water dubiously.

Ayesha caught her look. "It's okay I found an unopened bottle of water upstairs, it's fresh."

"Cool."

"What do we do first, he looks pretty beat up?"

"Hand I guess," Hannah flapped her hand towards the jug and cotton wool. "Get it cleaned up and then bandage it up I suppose."

Ayesha held up the water jug as Hannah grabbed three cotton wool balls and submerged them in the water for a second.

"Why the hell did they tie him up and torture him, you reckon?" Ayesha asked trying to open the green medicine box with her free hand without much luck.

"God knows. Maybe they were just trying to protect themselves and their home from people after their food or from the Infected. Guess we will never know now." Hannah squeezed out the cotton wool and began wiping the blood and grime off Matt's maimed left hand. Once most of the hand was clean and she took a deep breath before starting on the stubs of his fingers.

"No more, no more!"

They weren't sure who jumped more, Matt or the girls. As soon as the wet cotton wool had touched the remains of his missing fingers, Matt had jumped awake in pain and fright. Hannah and Ayesha both fell backwards, knocking over the jug of water, so they had to scramble back even more.

Hannah looked up, as Matt cradled his injured hand under the other, fear spread across his pale, drawn face. She felt sorry for him and what he had suffered. She knew he wasn't a perfect specimen of a man, but even he didn't deserve this kind of treatment.

"It's okay Matt, you are safe now," Hannah cooed.

"Those fuckers that hurt you are all dead now, the band is back together, man," Ayesha added.

Matt looked around the living room and then relaxed back into the sofa and began to sob.

"That's more like it, Judge eh," Tony said as he re-entered through the back door.

"What do you mean?" Selena looked up wearily from her mop. She and Ann had moved the table and remaining chairs over near the cooker. They had poured bleach and cleaning liquid into a bucket of water from the tap, to decontaminate it. As it was going onto the kitchen floor, they thought it would be safe enough. As long as nobody decided to eat their dinner off it, it should be fine.

"Men out in't fields, women in't kitchen cleaning up, where they belong," he said in a poor Yorkshire accent as he approached the wet, but clean kitchen floor.

"Don't you ever give it a fucking rest, man?" Selena said putting her mop into her bucket of pink water.

"Don't you come in here with those muddy boots on, take them the fuck off." Ann jumped in before her husband could reply and start another sexist row.

Tony raised his hand in submission. "Fair dues love. I was only trying to find where they kept their keys. There is a mini digger in the yard, thought I might bury the bastards and maybe burn the bodies too, just to make sure eh."

"Make sure of what?" Selena asked as Ann made her way over to a metal box fixed to a wall with a large number of keys inside.

"Make sure that after all this shit ends, we all don't get done for fucking murder, Judge. Get rid of the evidence."

Selena said nothing in reply. He had a good point. If law and order were resumed, they could all get sent to prison for a twenty stretch or longer for what they had done to survive.

"Here try these," Ann threw a set of keys with a red fob marked: _Digger_, over to her waiting husband.

"Cheers luv," Tony said as he caught the keys. "Later, ladies."

Ann and Selena watched as he left the farmhouse again.

"What shall we do with these," Ann prodded her bucket with her foot. "Down the sink?"

"Nah, better to throw them on the grass outside I think."

"Good idea, then I'll get some dinner going. Lucky they had

a wood burning Arga and not electric eh." Ann said as they picked up their buckets.

"Yes," Selena nodded and followed her outside. There were more women in the group than men, but she didn't like how they were settling down into certain gender roles. She didn't mind washing the floor as it had to be done, the hard work was cathartic after the terrible day they had endured. She had a cleaner and gardener at home, and she'd forgotten how menial tasks helped drive other worries from her mind. They had suffered an unprovoked attack, losing the gentle, loving Ellie in the fight. Such a senseless waste of life and then they had retaliated killing a whole family to satiate their bloodlust for revenge. She weighed the loss up and then thought of the girls who both had lucky escapes and then of Matt, maimed and imprisoned in the cellar. Did it all weigh up, one evil deed against the other? Was the law that she believed in for so many years now defunct in this new time of disease and death?

She was too tired to answer herself as they dumped the mops and buckets outside. Could she excuse the slaughter Tony, Ayesha, and Brita rained down on this farming family, was it defensible? At least they had fought and killed for a reason, for survival. She had killed someone because she was hurrying home to catch *MasterChef*. Her old life was gone; what use was a judge in times like these. She put her arm around Ann's neck in a gesture of female solidarity and they headed back into the kitchen.

As Ann headed for the pantry, happy to keep busy, Selena went to see how the rest of the group were getting on.

CHAPTER TWENTY-FOUR

THE SPOILS OF WAR

"Fuck me, it's colder than a witch's tit at dawn out there," Tony said coming in through the back door and pulling off the wellies he had borrowed. "That human fire it helped warmed me up a little, though."

Dusk was upon them, and everyone except Brita was in the kitchen or the living room and for two good reasons: they both had wood/coal burning fires. There was also another smaller room, with a boiler type fire that heated up the water and pipes around the house making it feel less cold. Selena and Ayesha had found the coal scuttle outside, it seemed they had plenty for a month at least and a woodshed that would last for a couple more months. The kitchen was toasty and warm, and Tony felt tired, hungry and a little light-headed as he entered. He kissed the top of Ann's head as he passed her at the cooker. He made for the pantry to have himself a can of Guinness, even though it was food in his belly his large frame really wanted.

"Dinner won't be long luv," Ann beamed at him, happy to be warm, dry and useful.

"Smells delish. Think we have fallen on our feet, this time, girls," he said as he pulled the top of his Guinness and drunk it before the golden foam could fall on the nice clean floor.

"We paid a heavy price for this comfort," Selena said to herself as she laid out plates for all around the cleaned kitchen table.

"But we paid them back with interest," Ayesha said. She sat on a far counter cleaning the blade of her axe with bleach and an old tea towel she had found in a cupboard.

"I'll drink to that," Tony tipped his can at her and downed nearly half the black brew.

Hannah wandered into the kitchen and threw some wipes and cotton wool in the bin.

"How's Matt now?" Selena asked standing up and feeling the muscles in her back. Mopping the floor had rediscovered back muscles that had rested dormant for years it seemed. They were awake again and in an angry mood.

"Resting up. I gave him some crackers and cheese, but even though he said he was hungry, he couldn't stomach much after I told him about Ellie." Hannah looked at the kitchen floor, glad it was free of blood.

"Shit, almost forgot that they had been an item too," Ann said lifting the lid of a boiling pan of greens to check them.

"Not good," Tony said with a slice of compassion that shocked the women in the room.

"How's Brita?" Hannah asked pulling up a chair to sit at the table.

"I checked on her twenty minutes ago, she wouldn't come down for food. She didn't say a word really. I told her about Matt, but no response. Poor thing." Selena told everyone.

"What about Ellie, she has to be buried doesn't she," Ann said taking the greens off the hotplate.

"Yeah, but not until its light," Hannah said.

"She can have one night with her, but then has to let her go. Tony can use the digger to dig her grave." Ayesha nodded to the big man, who took that moment to belch.

"Yeah, will need a digger too, bloody frost out there tonight already. Got to do it before she starts to pen n' ink too."

"Tony," Ann scolded her tactless husband.

"Well, it's bloody true. She can't stay up there until she goes off, she needs to be buried."

"Subtle as always Tony, that's Ellie we are talking about," Selena piped up.

"I know, but she is brown bread, and it's fucking shit cos she was the nicest girl, but facts are facts."

"I'll have a word with Brita," Ayesha said hopping off the

counter and putting aside her axe.

"Well, you can do it after dinner as it's ready now. Eat first and then you can take a drink and hot food up to Brita on a tray afterwards," Ann told her.

Ayesha nodded and took a seat next to Hannah at the kitchen table.

The rest of the group in the kitchen settled into chairs as Ann served up a glorious hot meal. Ann sat down, and they all tucked into the meal with gusto. Conversation halted as they filled their hungry bellies.

Matt picked up the cracker and got it as far as his split lips. The feel and smell of it made him feel sick, so he tossed it back onto the plate on the coffee table. He looked down at his bandaged left hand and fought back the urge to whimper over his missing digits. Yet, he had gotten off lightly compared with the two men he had thrown in with after the *Ramses Two* had got beached on that road. He had tagged along to the farm to get food and something safe to drink. He had nothing to do with raping that woman, but then again he had done nothing to stop it either. He had kept a poor watch outside the cattle shed. The sounds from inside both sickening him and giving him an iron hard erection at the same time. He had peeked once too often, not hearing the farmer and his sons approaching from behind.

Next thing he knew he woke up tied to the workbench in the cellar. He watched as the family took it in turns to torture and castrate one of his companions, the other they had shot on sight. Then she came down, fresh from a bath or shower and applied the final coup de grace on her rapist attacker. Then she had come at him with a pair of secateurs. He had protested his innocence, but that had not saved his pinkie finger. The next day she came down alone, wearing an angry scowl on her face and took his ring finger.

She had promised to visit every day and take a finger or maybe a toe until he had none left, making him feel as useless and helpless as she felt now.

Matt stood up and wiped the tears he was surprised to find on his cheeks. Selena had left someone to die, Ayesha and Tony had killed many people, and he had technically done nothing. He wiped his eyes again and thought of his poor Ellie. If he had not been stupid and cocky, having it off with one of his pupils, he would not be in this mess. He would have kept his eye on the ball with Ellie and not let her drift over to bat for the other side.

He left the room. The others were too busy eating to notice him head up the stairs. He had to try three different rooms before he found a dark, cold bedroom with two shapes lying together on one bed. One dead, one alive.

"Oh Eloise," he muttered as more tears of grief fell from his eyes this time.

A dark shape on the bed suddenly sat up, causing his heart to flutter in fear slightly.

"What do you want?" Brita's cold hard words emerged from the stygian darkness.

"To see her, and say my goodbyes. I loved her too you know."

"See what they did to her face, do you really want to see that, Matt. You are no man, no use and the love you gave her was false." Brita stood up, blocking the way to the bed. Some of her features showed, as Matt's eyes grew accustomed to the darkness.

"I know I let her down, but you didn't do a good job of protecting her either, did you?" He knew his words were a mistake before he even finished saying them. Brita rushed at him barging his back into the open door painfully. With an almost animalistic growl, she grabbed his T-shirt and twisted and shoved him out of the bedroom.

"She loved me, and I would have died for her," Brita snarled close-up into his face. "You are nothing but another weak man, full of desires but no passion. I hate you and all men like you. I cut the ropes to the *Ramses Two*, I set you adrift and hoped you would die. But cowards like you never die easy do they. Stay away from me, stay away from *my* Ellie, or I will gut you like a pig." Brita gave Matt a sidewards shove, he nearly fell, but ran off the stumble. He hurried downstairs without a look-back. He made it back to the sofa without anyone else noticing he had gone.

"I'll make you pay, you fucking bitch," he muttered under

his breath, as he picked up the cracker and crushed it in his right palm, wishing it was Brita's scrawny neck.

The hearty meal and overly warm kitchen had made most of the group sleepy. Tony took a bottle of brandy into the small boiler back room and drank half of it alone while Ann washed up. He didn't tell anyone, but he was trying to wipe the image of Ellie's exploding face from showing on a loop in his mind's eye. The brandy indeed helped, it sent him into a blissful dreamless sleep in front of the boiler.

Matt refused Hannah's offer of finding a bed upstairs for him. He took a spare pillow and a blanket but slept on the sofa that night. He was too scared to venture upstairs, anywhere near the deranged Brita lying next to his dead ex-fiancée.

"Shit. How can it be so toasty downstairs and so frigging freezing in the bedrooms," Ayesha said, only her eyes and nose showing from the covers of her bed.

"No central heating. Matt had the right idea sleeping in the living room," Hannah replied from her bed opposite. She had the covers up to her top lip and was curled up in a foetal position.

"How do you feel about Teacher-Boy being back babes?" Ayesha was sure she could see her breath like a cloud in front of her in the single candlelight.

"Not much. I'm glad he ain't dead I suppose. What about you?"

"What about me?"

"How do you feel about your *fuck-buddy* being back in the fold?"

"Don't bother me, but he ain't no use to me hun, I need a man with all his fingers if you get my meaning?"

"Ayesha!"

"Too soon?" Ayesha giggled.

"A bit," Hannah said, but she was smiling under her pulled up covers.

"I'm fucking bushed, night babes," Ayesha said turning over to face the window.

"Me too, night." Hannah reached out a hand from the warm covers to drag the candle on the bedside cabinet closer. The tiny hairs on her arms stiffened with the cold as she blew out the candle. Heavy darkness covered the room. It took her two hours to finally drift off. Her shoulders were hurting, and the images of blood and death pervaded her every thought, the second she closed her eyes. Fatigue took her in the end, but bad dreams soon followed.

Selena helped Ann wash and clear up because she felt guilty that the others had left her too it. They had thanked her for the meal, but neither teen nor her husband had offered to help her.

"I know we don't really get along, but thanks for helping out," Ann said as they put away the last of the plates.

"It's okay," Selena smiled at her. "Leave the pots to drip dry, I fancy a drink, how about you?"

Ann wiped her hot red forehead and threw her damp tea towel at the pots on the drainer. "Fuck it, why not, it's been a hell of a day."

"What do you fancy?" Selena asked as she opened the pantry door.

"I suppose a Malibu and coke is too much to ask for?"

"Erm." Selena clinked bottles as she looked through the booze supplies the late family hoarded in the pantry. She could not find what Ann was after, but grabbed a green bottle and a plastic one instead. "Gin and tonic?"

"Lots of gin and a dash of tonic for me please," Ann said sitting at the kitchen table. She spotted a drop of blood on the side of a placemat, so just put a salt pot in the way to hide it.

Selena placed the gin and tonic bottles on the table and went to a cupboard she had spotted earlier to grab two large tumblers. Selena poured out the gin for her and double the amount for Ann, with her delayed, "when."

Tonic Water followed, and the two other women of the group clinked their full glasses together.

"Cheers," Selena toasted.

"Bottoms up babe," Ann replied, and they both took a large gulp of their drinks. "That's better."

"Yes," Selena nodded.

The two women had not spent much time alone. Generally, Ann's ogre of a husband saw to that, and she couldn't think of a single thing to say to the woman.

Ann took another sip and was first to break the awkward silence. "You don't like me do you?"

"I wouldn't say that. After all these days together and all the things we have had to do to survive I feel I hardly know you, that's all." Selena sipped her drink again quickly.

"You hate my Tony."

"He's not my favourite type of man, no."

"You too good for the likes of my Tone and me then?"

"No," Selena shook her head and then met Ann's gaze for the first time. "I used to think I was back in my old life. But that was then, and this is now. I'm probably the worst of all of us. A hypocrite and a murderer. I have little skills to add to the group, I'm not an Amazon like Ayesha or Brita."

"You stand up to my Tony, that takes some balls, lady, I can tell you."

"Why don't you stand up to him more, you let him treat you like shit."

"Too fearful of a punch to the ribs or a backhander, it wears you down over the years. I know I shouldn't put up with it, but he is a strong, raw man. He protects me, he helps protect us all." Ann took another gulp.

"I know he has his uses, but real men don't need to scare or hurt the women they are supposed to love."

"It's okay for you with your big house, money, and powerful job. I'm just a dowdy, dumpy old housewife, but I tell you what, he has never cheated on me once."

"He has some redeeming qualities then?" Selena said, finishing her G&T, before pouring them both another.

"And if he did, he knows I'd cut his fucking nuts off at the root."

Selena laughed and Ann joined in as they clinked glasses once more.

"What do you reckon we should do now?" Selena asked as the laughter died away.

"Why ask me?"

"Because I don't think anyone ever does ask you, that's why."

"I dunno, stay here I suppose, at least for the time being. It's warm, we have lots of food. And that back boiler will heat the water too, so a hot bath sounds a luxury to me. I'm tired of wandering about with no real destination. Winter isn't far off."

"See, your opinion is worth its weight in gold, Ann, you should speak up more often."

"You want to stay here then or head for the coast? It might be just as shit there, or even worse, we could get there and there is nothing but dead and Infected people."

"I think we should stay here for a few days at least. Rest up, bury poor Ellie and then all vote to see what our next course of action is. Take our time."

"Poor Ellie, she was too good for this world. We gave our best to secure this farm, we should stay here."

"To the spoils of war then," Selena said raising her glass.

"What you said." They toasted and drank more gin.

CHAPTER TWENTY-FIVE

THE BURIAL

Tony was first to wake. The armchair he had slept in had given him aching pains in his kidney area. Technically, Brita was the first up, because she never slept a wink. The grey light through the thin curtain showed the rigid remains of her Ellie, covered in a bloody white sheet. She felt for life in her lover's hand, but it was as cold and icy as the bedroom they occupied. She somehow found more tears to weep, turning away from Ellie's corpse to stare at the curtains.

The throbbing in Matt's left hand woke him next. He swallowed some painkillers Hannah had found in a bathroom cabinet upstairs and washed them down with the flat remains of a can of coke he had started last night. He cradled his left hand to his chest, squeezing his wrist to try and stem the throbbing, but it didn't help at all. He ate the remains of his crumbled stale cracker and then left the living room for the kitchen, in search of more food.

Hannah woke with a cold nose and the remnants of nightmares circling like vultures in her brain. She needed to pee, the urge heightened as soon as her bare feet touch the cold wooden floorboards. She raced to the bathroom, seeing the window was all frosted up outside.

"Shitty day for a funeral," she stated to the shower curtain as she sat down to pee.

Ayesha, Ann, and Selena had the best night's sleep out of the lot of them. Ann mainly because her snoring afflicted husband had spent the night downstairs in the boiler room. She rubbed her bare arms and went into the en-suite of the master bedroom to quickly wash her face and dress. The water from the hot tap was too hot to hold her hands under. Ann eyed the nearby bath. "Why the fuck not," she said and put in the plug to have her first hot bath in ages. The sight of hot water pouring from the taps was a sight to behold, and she scrabbled around under the sink to pour some bubble bath in too. Such simple pleasures were the ones you missed most.

Ann stripped off naked as the warmth from the enticing bath heated the en-suite. A bath rather than a shower meant these people had good taste in Ann's eyes. She turned on the cold tap and then stared down at herself. She saw a sight that rocked her back on her heels.

Selena held her breath and then knowing she could wait no longer, she just went for it. She went for her pack unzipped a pocket to reveal her version of the *Holy Grail* and *Golden Fleece* and the *Ark of the Covenant* all rolled into one: her last saved pair of clean knickers. She whipped down one pair and pulled on the clean ones. She still had her socks on from bed and a t-shirt. She sprayed her pits through the arm holes and jumped into her jeans and tugged on her pullover.

All done in less than forty-five seconds. She breathed out, forming a cloud in the icy air of the bedroom. Selena tugged on her boots, her cold fingers having trouble with the laces. Then she hurried downstairs and prayed for some warmth. The ambient temperature downstairs was warmer than upstairs, but all the fires had turned to cold ash. Tony passed her head down grumbling, heading upstairs, without a good morning to her. Not that she had given him the time-of-day either.

Selena stood in the hall and tapped her top lip, pondering which fire to rekindle first. As most people would gravitate towards the kitchen when they got up, she decided to make that her first priority. She was in desperate need for a nice cup of tea, to clear her head and take the taste of gin from her tongue. She swung her head around the living room door to check on Matt, he waved at her from the sofa with his good hand. Then made for the kitchen to light the Arga.

"I can see my bush," Ann stated in amazement as she looked down her body. If she breathed in she could see her pubic hair, a sight long covered by her large breasts and belly. Both had reduced. The more she looked around at her naked self, the more weight loss she noticed, in her thighs, arms, and bum.

Amidst the ruins of the world, she smiled. "Only took the end of the world to make me lose my lard," she mused. "The bloody bath." Ann had forgotten the water and turned off the cold tap before it could undo all the nice steaming hot water she had put in. She put her hand in the water and wiggled it about, just right. She had put her foot up on the edge of the bath, when the master bedroom door was barged open.

"Ann?" Came the grumpy call of her mate and her heart sank a little.

"I'm in here, about to have a bath," she called through the bathroom door. She eased her right foot into the bubble layered water and sighed from her toes to her head as it sunk inside. She was about to follow it with her left when the door crashed open, nearly off its hinges and ducking inside Tony grabbed her naked body around the waist and dragged her from the bath and back into the bedroom. "What the fuck is wrong with you, I was only taking a bath!"

Tony unceremoniously threw his wife onto the bed knocking the breath from her lungs. "What the fuck are you doing you stupid moronic cow!"

He towered over her, a simmering bulk of menace.

"I just wanted to feel clean, you prick!"

"Where the fuck does the water come from, is it safe? We don't drink the water because it could be contaminated with that Red Death shit and you want to fucking wallow in that you fucking idiot. Think," he shouted prodding her forehead with his large forefinger.

"I... didn't think," she whispered back. He wasn't mad at her, he wasn't after rough sex, he was trying to save her life, she realised. "Sorry."

"Get the fuck dressed and get me some breakfast, I've got a

bloody hangover if you want to thank me," he said hands on his hips breathing hard.

Ann suddenly felt the cold of the bedroom and hurried to get dressed, while Tony drained the bath. She held back her tears in front of him like she always tried to do. It only made him more tense and angry. She sobbed on the stairs, mopped her eyes in the hallways and was her usual self by the time she made it into the kitchen. Selena looked up from lighting the Arga, and Ann smiled back at her. She hid her pain, behind that smile for so many years, it was easy.

There was a heavy frost. So the digger was required to scoop up the hard earth for Ellie's grave. The group, apart from Brita, shared a warm breakfast in the kitchen. Selena, Ayesha and Tony had found a spot on a sunny rise of the hill, in the top end corner of a field by a large ancient Alder tree. Ayesha carried one of the shotguns as she eyed the fields. Something bothered her about the farm, but she did not realise it until the burial had got underway. Where were all the livestock?

They were all gathered round the grave. Ann had made a wreath out of laurel, ivy and other green plants with orange berries. The last warm days of autumn were over it seemed, and winter was suddenly upon them. The sky was blue, and the sun was out, but a bitter wind blew up from the south to the high exposed area by the tree and fence. Hannah escorted Brita, walking behind her in a thick blue coat she had found in a wardrobe. Brita was dressed in all black. DMs dark combat trousers and a black bomber jacket she had found in the men's wardrobe of the bedroom she and Ellie had lain in all night. Her hair was scraped back and her pale face exposed to the winds, chapping her already dry lips. She looked pale as a ghost to Hannah as the Danish woman carried Ellie up the rise to the open grave. Brita had sown Ellie into the sheet she was covered with, like sailors of old. The red blood stain around the head a vivid, marked contrast to the white covers. The other hurried to help her as she neared the grave, but she shook her head tight-lipped and silent. The look in her cold blue eyes made them back away from the grave again.

Tony had only dug the grave four feet deep, making it easier
for Brita to lay her lover's legs in first, followed by her body
and then gently reached down to let her head rest on the cold
earth at the bottom. Brita stood and walked silently to the foot
of the grave and looked down upon her love's body. She had not
prepared for this moment or had any idea of what to say, until
now. A poem her grandfather had taught her as a child came to
mind.

"I Barndommens lange og dunkle Nat brænder smaa
blinkende Lygter som Spor, af Erindringen efterladt, mens
Hjertet fryser og flugter." She said in her native tongue.
"What's she saying?" She heard Ann whisper to Selena next to
her around the grave.

"It is a poem. In childhood's long night, both dim and dark;
there are small twinkling lights that burn bright, like trace
memory's left there as sparks. While the heart freezes and takes
flight."[1]

"Beautiful," Hannah said beside her.

"I loved you so much, my Ellie, until we meet again." Brita
picked some hard brown earth from the pile beside the grave
and threw it onto the sheet covered corpse. "Thank you,"
she said to the gathering and turned and walked back to the
farmhouse.

Hannah looked at the others and pointed asking silently if
she should follow. Selena and Ann shook their heads. Next to
them Matt sank to his knees and began to weep loudly for his
lost fiancée. Hannah supposed he had a right to feel upset, but
it made her feel sick. So much so she had to hurry around the
tree and throw up her breakfast. Ayesha ran around the tree to
pat her back.

"You okay?"

"Yeah feel better now," Hannah said wiping her chin with
her coat sleeve.

"Something you ate?"

Hannah looked at her, a rude joke forming in her mind, but

---

1   Tove Ditlevsen, from 1947
Blinkende Lygter

this wasn't the time. "I think it could be morning sickness?"

"Let's get you back to the farmhouse and out of this ruddy cold," Ayesha said, draping a friendly arm around her shoulder. Hannah just nodded in agreement. Selena was trying to comfort Matt while Ann and Tony began to shovel the earth over Ellie's body before it froze solid. They worked quickly, glad of the warmth hard work gave and the sooner they were finished the sooner they could get back to the warm farmhouse.

"So, where do you reckon all the cows or sheep or ducks this place keeps have gone?" Ayesha asked Hannah as they trudged back down the hill past the large closed animal sheds.

"Ducks?"

"Do I look like a girl who knows about farming and shit?"

"No." Hannah shook her head. "I dunno, maybe in one of those big barn buildings?"

"Yeah, but wouldn't we have heard them mooing or stuff?"

"I suppose. We could take a look now; I don't feel too bad now I've vomed."

"Fuck off, its way too cold mate, and besides its wake time so we need to get alcohol down our necks. It's tradition."

"You can do the drinking for two while I do the eating for two," Hannah said with a thin smile.

"You get fat, and I get wasted double time." Ayesha nodded. "I can live with that arrangement, babes."

Brita was nowhere to be found downstairs when they got back, but they heard her moving about upstairs so did not worry. Ayesha set about making a pot of tea, with Hannah sitting, giving out instructions. If it did not plug in, vibrate or go ping, Ayesha did not know how to use it.

Brita locked the bathroom door behind her and used the chair in the bathroom to wedge under the handle to make sure. She ran the bath, hoping the sound did not carry downstairs to the kitchen. As both taps spilt what was left in the pipes and tanks, she opened the three doors of the bathroom cabinet and searched through them. She picked up a pink plastic razor but then saw something even better in the third one. She grabbed it and dropped the razor into a nearby bin. She held her prize tight in her left hand as she stripped naked. Brita folded her black clothes and left them on the toilet seat. Placing the boots on top last. She turned off the taps and tested the water. It was warm enough. She stepped into the bath and sat down. Even in her traumatised state of grief, she relished the warm water as it covered her legs and lower body. She lowered her head under the water, as her bent knees broke the surface. Holding her breath for twenty seconds and then pushed herself up out of the hot water again.

Only then did she open her tight closed palm. She looked at the cutthroat razor, before releasing its sharp blade and setting to work with it.

The rest of the group sat in the kitchen, drinking beer, wine and spirits, but not really enjoying the tastes and warming flavours. Nobody spoke, not even Tony made any rude or annoying remarks. Ellie had been the bright, delicate heart of the group that everyone liked/loved and wanted to protect. Everyone had changed since the Red Death, and the floods had destroyed their lives. They had toughened, become more savvy and cruel to survive; yet Ellie had remained the same, like a link to their past lives, and now she was gone.

No one left the warm kitchen. Even though there were fractious factions between those who remained, they knew they were safer together than being alone. Matt had shown them that fact and had two missing fingers to prove it. Ayesha was the first to move after an hour. She hopped off the counter, put down her wine and grabbed one of the shotguns resting against the small partition wall that led to the back door.

"Where are you going with that?" Selena asked her, as Ayesha put four spare cartridges in her coat pocket.

"Something that is nagging me, I mentioned it to Han earlier. This is a farm right, but I ain't seen any animals. So I'm going to check the sheds and barns or whatever they are called and do a sweep of the place, check for Infected."

"Want company?" Matt asked turning in his chair.

"Nah, you're alright," Ayesha turned and left the muted wake.

Hannah wanted to stand up and rush out after her, but the warm kitchen was making her feel a little sick again.

"Got some balls that one now," Tony muttered into a stein he had found hanging on a hook to quaff his Guinness.

"I'm going to check on Brita," Hannah said, using it as an excuse to leave the overly warm kitchen.

"Tell her we are thinking of her," Ann called after her. Tony grunted into his beer but said nothing.

The rest of the downstairs was still warm, but more tolerable. It wasn't until Hannah was halfway up the stairs did the heat get sucked away, and the cold enveloped her. But it felt good, for the time being. Her nausea disappeared almost immediately. She pulled down the sleeves of her pullover and stood outside Brita's room. Hannah raised her knuckles to the door and knocked after a slight pause.

"Brita, are you okay?"

She heard nothing, so took a step back from the door. She waited for a reply, but none came. She knocked again. A little more venom in her raps on the wooden bedroom door. Hannah wondered what she would want at this time, to be alone or to know people cared about her. She decided on the latter and turned the knob, to reveal an empty room. A sucking noise from the bathroom, caused her to spin round and head in that direction.

"Brita are you in there. Sorry to intrude, are you okay?" Hannah's hand hovered over the door handle. She heard a sucking sound, like water running from a bath. Wouldn't the bath water be contaminated?

Hannah pulled down on the handle and entered the bathroom. Her hands went to her mouth in shock when she saw Brita. "Brita what have you done?"

Ayesha found if she broke the shotgun and put it over her shoulder, it was less heavy to lug around. There were three enormous buildings around the farm, so Ayesha went for the nearest one. She pulled open one of the sliding double doors to reveal a long and clean milking shed. There were rows on each side where individual cows could be milked. The place smelt of off-milk and hospitals. She closed the door and moved around the side past a locked Farm shop, that she knew they should search sometime soon. Across a concrete road area was one of two very tall barns, she assumed. To the left were sheds and garages for the tractors and digger. She ignored them and moved to the first barn. She opened it up with a grunt of effort. It seemed to Ayesha to be like a big aircraft hangar, with a wide concrete road down the middle with furrows of hay on either side. Then two gated off pens where the cows were kept in the winter or overnight. The place smelt vaguely of a hamster hutch she once had as a kid in her bedroom.

The place was silent, vast and empty.

Ayesha frowned and left the barn heading through the farmyard past some smaller birthing sheds. The second vast cow shed lay away in the north-east corner of the farm and nearer the large fields that sloped gently down the hill from the levelled out farm area. She was only halfway there when a new farmyard smell assaulted her nostrils. Like manure and roast beef dinners. The shed was open and empty as the last, but the smell was stronger. She readied the shotgun with a click and walked briskly around it to find a large gate in a frost tinged hedge. When she got to the gate and looked into the field, the teenager stopped dead. The sloping fields of grass were blocked from view from the place they buried Ellie, by the two tall barns.

In a level dip in the field, there were four immense bonfires. Burnt down to ash and bones and inside were the remains of the hundreds of cows the farmers once owned. Ayesha could see some of the cattle were still recognisable while others were twisted blackened shapes. Each bonfire had been thirty feet across at least. Yet that wasn't the worst of it.

Shuffling through the carcases and ash were five Infected, munching down on the burnt offerings. They hadn't noticed her, so Ayesha crept back from the gate and then ran back to the farmhouse to inform the others.

CHAPTER TWENTY-SIX

DIGGING IN

"Brita?"

Brita stood before Hannah, her pale flesh clinging to her athletic body. Her lovely white-blonde locks had been shaved off to reveal a bald plate underneath, with the odd scar and blue vein to give her an almost alien look. She was shaven everywhere apart from her almost blonde-white eyebrows. Hannah realised how much a woman's hair affected the beauty of their face. Brita looked awkward, and it made her thin lips look cruel.

Hannah picked up a towel off a rail and drew it around Brita's cold shoulders. "Why did you do this to yourself?" she whispered.

"Ellie loved playing with my hair," Brita stated without making eye contact with Hannah.

"So why did you chop it all off, it looked so lovely."

"Because she is gone forever. I have no need to look pretty anymore. It is cold in here now."

"Let's get you dressed then eh," Hannah said moving the black DMs off her clothes to dress her.

Brita did not resist her, neither did she help her. Under the clothes was a black hoodie, borrowed from one of the wardrobes in Brita's bedroom. Hannah pulled it up over her head to keep it warm. She led her to the stairs.

"Where are we going?" Brita asked her in a dull voice like she was some speak your weight automaton.

"Downstairs, it's nice and warm down there. Get you

something to eat or drink." Hannah coaxed Brita's feet into motion down the stairs. "Selena," Hannah called when she rounded the stair banister and entered the hallway.

Selena stood up from her seat at the table and hurried to help Hannah take Brita by the elbow and guide her into the kitchen. All chatter between Ann, Tony and Matt died instantly at seeing the frail looking Danish woman.

"She looks weird," Tony said in his usual subtle manner. "Why?"

"Brita what have you done to yourself?" Ann hurried forwards to help guide the grief-stricken woman to a chair at the kitchen table. "I'll fetch you something to eat."

"I cut my hair, that is all," Brita said in her monotone voice.

"Fuck me, the daft cow has shaven her head, proper lesbian now she looks with those boots on," Tony said, even he was shocked how frail she suddenly looked. Not that he cared at all.

Matt did not look at her at all. In fact, he stood to leave.

The backdoor burst open and made everyone except Brita jump. Tony hurried over to pick up the other shotgun and then saw who it was racing into the kitchen at a rate-of-knots. Ayesha left the back door open, letting in the cold from outside.

"We've got company in the back field," Ayesha panted trying to catch her breath.

"People company?" Selena asked.

"No, the Infected kind… at least five of the fuckers. Chewing down on the crispy cows."

"Crispy cows?" Hannah frowned.

"Yeah, I found all the cows. They burnt every single one of them. Come on, we gotta go sort them out."

"Maybe to stop the infection spreading," Selena mused as she pulled on her coat.

Ayesha turned and was moving to the doors as Tony grabbed one of the large farmer's coats for himself. "Ann, you stay here with her," he pointed at Brita.

"I'm fucking coming with you," Brita stood up and grabbed Pier's fireman's axe.

"I'm coming," Matt said standing up.

"Well I ain't going to be left on my own," Ann said loudly.

"Well, fucking hurry your fat arse up then," Tony shouted, bustling after Ayesha out the back door. In the end, they all wrapped up for the cold and left the farmhouse.

The whole group hurried across the road into the farmyard. Tony stopped and waved them on, "I'll catch up with you lot in a jiffy."

Ann followed the rest of the group up to the corner of the farm, to the wide metal fence in the hedgerow.

"Shit," Matt said seeing the mounds of burnt cattle and the Infected milling around the carcasses looking for easy pickings.

"What shall we do, shoot them?" Ann asked peering over the hedge. The Infected were so engrossed in filling up on the cooked beef, they did not notice the group at all.

"I suppose," Hannah said, looking around. "Where's your Tony and the other shotgun?"

"Wait, what's that noise?" Selena said.

Then they saw the second tractor which had been next to the digger roaring around the second cow shed and made a bee-line for the gate. "Open the gates!" Tony called from inside.

Selena and Ann did as he said, as he roared the tractor into life and down into the field. The Infected had noticed them and left their easy pickings to go after the group. They had Tony and the tractor to deal with now. His first run smashed two of the Infected to the ground, one squashed under the tyres. He continued on to hit another dead on, turning its head into jelly. Then he rounded on the two that were left, heading up the hill towards the group. They were six feet apart so he swung the bouncing tractor around in a wide arc and ran across them from the side, squashing one flat and clipping the other to the floor. Brita ran forwards and cut off the head of the clipped Infected as it struggled to rise from the slippery frozen grass.

Tony pulled up the tractor by the hedge, next to the open fence.

Brita's hood had slipped off as she had gone in for the coup-de-grace. Tony got out of the tractor cab, as Brita trudged up the hill to where the others waited.

"Well done Kojak," Tony shouted over to her; triumphantly pleased with his murderous efforts. He raised the shotgun in the air in victory. "No need to waste a single shot either."

Brita ignored him and handed the axe back to Ayesha, who had to juggle the shotgun to accept it.

"We need to dig in and make this place secure like," he said as he rejoined the others.

"We staying then?" Ann said, giving him a victory hug.

"We fucking are, dunno about you lot, but it's getting too bloody cold to be trampling around the countryside and sleeping rough. We took this place in battle like, so it's ours now by rights."

"The ancient law of finders-keepers eh," Selena said in a mocking tone, but he didn't catch on.

"Yeah, something like that."

"Can we go back inside, this cold is agony on my hand," Matt suggested, and they all went back to the warm farmhouse again.

"What if the police or army finally turn up, what do we say? We murdered the family that owned this farm and took it for ourselves?" Selena continued.

"What police, what army? Ain't no one coming to save us Judge and if you don't like it, well you don't have to stay," Tony replied.

Selena didn't have a reply for this. She knew that this was where she belonged now, amongst killers and thieves because she was one of them.

"If we are staying we need to make plans," Hannah said later that night around the dinner table.

"What sort of plans?" Ayesha asked, reaching over to grab a knife.

"To defend this place, make it more secure eh," Tony butted in.

"Well...yeah, but we need fresh water to survive the winter. We won't live long without it, and we can't trust the taps or getting it from rivers just in case it is contaminated."

"Where we going to get it from girl?" Tony leant back in his chair and let out a loud yawn.

"We could set up water butts to collect rainwater and then

boil it. Also, check all the houses in the village when the flood waters recede for bottled water and cans," Hannah explained her point.

"We could take the tractor, with a trailer hooked up, to other villages to stock up on food and water," Ann suggested.

"That's doable," Tony nodded, patting his wife condescendingly on the top of her head.

"The only problem I foresee with that is, the larger the area of civilisation we visit the more risk we have of attack by Infected," Selena said stirring her hot soup.

"And we might find other normal people, who don't want to share," Ayesha pointed out.

"Then water butts everywhere, boil everything but bottled water, search local villages first when the waters have gone down. How are we for food, Ann?" Hannah looked over at Tony's wife.

Ann was a little taken aback, she had taken on the duties of cook, but wasn't used to someone asking her opinion on anything. She smiled nervously at Hannah and then replied. "The farmers who were here before us must have bought food in bulk. We have loads of boxes and tins of food, racks of the stuff in the pantry."

"Enough to last a couple of months?" Selena inquired.

"Enough to last all winter but like Hannah says the water situation is the problem, we will run out in less than a fortnight, tops," Ann said, getting the hang of owning an important role in the group. Before she had been a hanger-on and Tony's wife, now she had a warm feeling of self-worth.

"Then we need to start conserving water and supplementing our supply pretty fast. That will be our group task for tomorrow, finding water butts, troughs and barrels around the farm to collect together near the farmhouse. Agreed?"

Everyone agreed with Selena's suggestion.

"Knowing our luck it won't rain again for weeks," Ayesha laughed, and Tony, Matt, and Hannah joined in.

A gale force wind hampered their efforts the next day. The wind-chill factor dipped into the blue and even forced the resilient Tony back inside for frequent tea breaks and to warm up. Wheelie bins to troughs to empty barrels were aplenty around the farm, and they placed them on the lawn next to the farmhouse's back door. Brita found chicken wire and some old sieves to place over the various twenty or so containers to keep out the leaves that had suddenly started to shed from the trees. She doubled and then tripled up the covers, to stop wild animals drinking from them. Hannah had found some special disinfectant that the farmers used on the milking machines, to wash them out.

They were all teary-eyed and had raw cheeks from the wind by the time they had finished and were glad to get inside the warmth again. The kitchen had become the central hub of the house, and it was usually the warmest place to be.

"There are two houses really near we can check out tomorrow for supplies," Ayesha said as they tucked into a hearty meal of tinned chicken curry.

"Yeah, we need to check them out, I don't mind doing that," Tony said, wiping curry sauce off the beard forming on his chin, as he scarfed his food down like it was his last meal.

"We can take the shotguns and check them out," Matt suggested.

"Maybe we should keep one here at all times," Selena pointed out.

"Why?" Matt said, his loaded fork paused between his plate and his open mouth.

"We have lots of supplies here. Supplies that the farmers attacked us to protect. We need to do the same. Have someone on a rota to guard the farm, while some of us go out scavenging. We can take it in turns who goes out," Selena suggested.

"Makes sense," Hannah said.

"Well, I'll lead the group to look for stuff," Tony jumped in. "I'll take Ayesha, you, Judge and the lezza."

"What about me?" Matt piped up.

"And me?" Hannah said, in a bit too teen whiney voice.

Ann looked relieved in not being asked along. Brita took little notice of anything since Ellie had died.

"Well, you've only got one hand so you can't carry shit and

she's up the duff. I need fighters and carriers with me," Tony burped and then ate the remains of his curry.

"What am I supposed to do all day then?" It was Matt's turn to sound like a spurned whiney teenager.

"Well you can help my Ann do the washing up, and women's work and your gymslip schoolgirl here can have the shotgun as she has more sack than you ever will soppybollocks."

"Fuck you," Matt said, then realised what he had said and to whom and left the table in a hurry.

"In ya, dreams mate. You maybe have shagged half the group, but my arse ain't out for rent," Tony bellowed after the fleeing Matt, followed by deep fits of his own laughter.

The women at the table looked at each other, shook their heads but said nothing.

"More curry luv?" Ann offered the remains of the pot to her husband. Nobody had the energy to object to the nepotism on who got second helpings. As long as it shut Tony up for a while.

"Don't mind if I fucking do hun." Tony held up his plate for more.

The large house down the lane was empty of people, Infected or otherwise. It showed signs of people leaving in a hurry and the double garage was open and empty. Tony's scavenger group took everything from the house that could be of use and put it in the trailer affixed to the back of the tractor. Outside was a large organic garden, which was a big bonus. They found carrots and parsnips still in the ground and apples still in the trees. They took the best ones they could find. The gales of yesterday had taken most of the apples off the trees anyway. They only had to contend with a slight cold easterly breeze today.

The second home was a bust. There was a family of five Infected inside, locked in tight. Even Tony thought the risks of disturbing them, would outweigh any supply gains they would get. The house was down the lane and far enough away to pose an acceptable risk to the farmhouse. That afternoon Brita went missing for an hour. Half n' hour after her return, they could see the black smoke pluming into the sky from the house's general direction. Nobody said a word to Brita, she hardly listened

to what the rest of the group said anymore. She went into a
dark, lonely place and only spoke in Danish to any question
posed to her.

A week went by, and they saw no signs of anyone. The flood
waters in the nearby village lowered so they could see the mud
caked church and houses from two of the bedroom windows of
the farmhouse. Leaving only Hannah behind with one of the
shotguns, they left the farmhouse in the tractor and a Range
Rover and headed down into the village. A light dusting of
snow lay across the rooftops and surrounding fields.

Hannah waved them off and went back inside to boil some
overnight snow water they had collected. The air was icy, and
the sun was low and dazzling off the windshields and mirrors
of the vehicles as they drove down the muddy lane into the village in the valley below.

CHAPTER TWENTY-SEVEN

THE VILLAGE

A low mist hovered over the edges of the small valley. Frost gave the snow a Crème Brule top crust as the scavenging group left the safety of their vehicles. The ice and light snow covered the worst of the mudslides and remains of the flood waters were thick ice ponds. The village was only a couple of minutes' ride or a ten-minute walk from the farm, but topography was the key. The farm on the top of the rise of the valley had not been affected much at all by the floods, while the village only thirty feet lower had been devastated. The local village stream that ran the length of the north side of the village had been the focal point for the floods.

Some of the houses on slight rises had fared better than others but had still had waterlogged downstairs. The other older lower houses had been submerged to their first-floor windows, and any bungalows had vanished beneath the waters. The waters had gone, but had left behind cars, rubbish, trees, cattle, and the odd human corpse entombed in muddy graves. A lower road to the left ran down into such a hell of Mother Nature's rage that it was impassable. They parked outside the local church on a less flood affected road. Steps led up to the soggy remains of the graveyard. The sign that proclaimed the St. Nicholas's church had remained intact, but some of the graves had sunken away under the weight of the flood waters to show rotten coffins and skeletal remains of the local parishioners long deceased.

"Where do we start?" Matt surveyed the area from the top

of the steps. His left arm was in a sling as his maimed hand throbbed less in that position.

"You are the geography teacher; you tell us?" Selena said pulling up the hood of her coat to keep out the cold.

"Thanks." Matt puffed out his cheeks. "Maybe if we can get into that bell tower, we can see the lay of the land. Try and spot a post office or local shop or pub would be good for water and supplies."

"Betcha all the good stuff is buried under shit, mud or water," Ayesha said, stamping her feet to keep warm.

"Let's get out of this fucking cold wind," Tony said joining Matt on the path leading up to the thick grey-walled church. "See if the vicar kept a supply of communal wine and dirty mags in his vestry."

Selena shook her head but followed him. Brita brought up the rear in silence, carrying a wood cutting axe she had found at the farm. She and Ayesha looked like they had escaped a lumberjack's convention. They followed a slippery path up to the porch-like entrance to the imposing church. Apart from a few crows screeching to each other from a nearby elm, the village was silent as the graves that surrounded them.

"I don't like this," Ann said, "it's creepy."

"We have to start somewhere, why not this lovely twelfth-century church, with its thirteenth and fourteenth-century additions to its size and architecture," Selena said, craning her neck to take in the roof of the church.

"How do you know all this stuff?" Ayesha asked her with a shrug.

"Was a hobby of mine many years ago, when I still had time for such frivolous time wastes. Now I know my career was the real waste of my time."

"What you mean?" Ayesha pressed, as Tony tried the door.

"I got high up, earning loads of money, but I was alone in my big house. Now I realise it's not money, career or material things that makes one happy, but the people you share your life with that count."

Ayesha gave the older woman a brief hug through their respective bulky coats.

"There we go," Tony said, putting a crowbar Matt had brought with him to good use on the locked porch door. With his extra weight and strength, the wooden frame of the door next to the lock broke, and the door juddered inwards. "Easy."

He and Matt swapped weapons and moved inside the main nave area of the gloomy church. Grabbing the shotgun, Tony ventured two steps inside. There was a gap between wooden pews to his left, right and in front. He immediately saw that he was not alone; the church pews had lying, sitting figures dotted all around. Thirty or so his mind quickly calculated. Then he noticed the gait and movement of the figures as they began to rise and notice his presence. He saw the gnawed bones on the stone aisle leading up to the chancel and altar. Then, at last, his mind registered that the people inside who had become so interested in his intrusion were all faceless Infected.

"Fuck it," he whispered and tried to back up out of the church only to bump into Matt behind him. They had noticed him. A wasted creature sat up from the nearest pew near the doorway and raked at him with her ruined fingers. Lucky for Tony, her nails had long since dropped off and he poked her back hard with the barrels of the shotgun before backing out of the church. He pulled the now useless door shut and turned to look at the rest of the bemused scavengers. "Infected!"

The group scattered into two separate parties, as the church door was wrenched open by desperate, bloody hands. Tony fired once into the dead centre of the following group before he turned and ran. His shot took off the side of the head of one Infected and knocked down two others following behind. He followed the nearest person, who was Matt. Only when he turned to see the Infected pouring from the church like ants from a disturbed nest, did he realise that Ann, with Ayesha and Selena were separated from him running for the vehicles. The twenty or more Infected were between him and that entrance, all he could do was heave his bulky frame after Matt and the fleeing Brita before him.

Lucky for him the Infected were weakened from their disease, condition and lack of sustenance from being locked up in the church. He turned and fired low at the gaining pack behind him. Already bloody kneecaps were shredded, and two Infected took a tumble taking two more with them. He weaved through the grave and tombs after the much younger and fitter Brita and Matt. His legs were burning, but he knew a month ago he wouldn't have got this far. The weight had dropped off him, but thoughts of that and his hopes that Ann had gotten to the cars and out of the village were forefront in his mind.

Every breath was a pain to his lungs and knees, as first Brita and then Matt disappeared through a hole in a high hedge. He ran after them, trampling over a fallen gate, which was the boundary between the graveyard and the once tended lawn of a large house. He thought he heard a car drive off at high speed as he peaked over his shoulder. The Infected were more decrepit than he thought and were at least ten feet behind. He saw Matt round the rear of the large red brick house and followed him round the shingle path that encircled the home.

With his lungs feeling like he had inhaled liquid fire, he was just in time to see the back door slam shut and Matt began to beat on it with his one good fist. Tony had to slow to a jog as he broke the shotgun and pulled out the spent cartridges. He fumbled in his coat pocket for more. He managed to bring out four but lost two from his shaking hands. He loaded up as Matt banged and kicked at the locked back door.

"Brita for pity's sake let us in," he shouted at the sturdy looking backdoor.

The vanguard of the chasing Infected group appeared around the corner, making Tony lock the shotgun and fire off a hasty first shot. It took half a corner brick from the side of the house but nailed one poor creature in the throat and slightly deterred the others. Tony looked at the windows, but they were all shut, more Infected poured around the corner and he fired again taking off arms and legs of two of the closing pack. Yet more replaced them and he knew he and Matt were in a dire situation.

"Come on," Ayesha almost pulled Ann down the steps of the church towards the range rover.

"What about my Tony?" Ann wailed, as Ayesha raced ahead with the car keys.

"He can take care of himself, so can the others, but we need to go," Ayesha screamed in her face. A group of ten Infected were chasing after them. The majority of the residents of the church went after the other part of their group. Selena had got the car open and jumped into the driver's seat. Ayesha opened the door behind Selena and pushed Ann roughly inside and jumped in after her, nearly catching her long hair in the door as she slammed it shut.

Selena started the engine and central locked all the doors as the first of the more mobile Infected reached her door. The sight of their wide lidless yellowed orb-like eyes and lipless teeth and bleeding gums pressing against the glass pumped even more adrenaline through her body. Ignoring the faces, hands leaving bloody smears on her window, she put the Range Rover into gear and sped off down the road knocking down three Infected as she moved off. She glanced in the rear-view mirror as she gained some distance and noticed the last few Infected looked weak and almost on the point of collapse. She sped past the local village pub and slowed to a stop at the T-junction ahead.

Looking left the road dipped down into the rest of the lower parts of the village. A trailer was half skewed across the road, forming a mud bank across most of that way.

Looking right the road was clear and that was the general direction the others had been running. She indicated out of habit and turned right and sped along the road to see what she could see. Trees and hedges forming the boundary of the graveyard sped past. A break in the greenery brought a large red brick house into view. The three women inside the car could see the line of Infected from the church heading around the side of the large building. The drive of the large house was barred by a solid looking thick wooden gate, but another open drive with brick walls only a little way ahead showed promise.

"Where are we going?" Ayesha yelled, grabbing a roof handle as Selena skidded the Range Rover at high speed into the next open driveway. Low brick walls gave way to some open large equestrian centre. The large house lined with old stables behind was connected with the centre and a local business park. So she skidded the vehicle to a stop and then slammed on the horn.

The foreign bitch wasn't going to open the door. Tony grabbed Matt and pulled him with him around the back of the house hoping to find somewhere else to hide. The garden and path led to a long low block of wooden stables, so they ran as fast as their tired bodies could handle. A loud car horn blared out somewhere unseen but close by ahead of them. It spurred them on, even though Tony had a wicked stitch in his left side. The Infected stumbled relentlessly after them. They rounded the green moss covered roofed stable to find the Range Rover waiting for them, horn blaring out again. They half-jogged/half walked over to the waiting vehicle. Tony could see the relieved face of Ann in the back seat waving him closer. Tony got in the back as Ann and Ayesha scooched over while Matt got in next to Selena.

"Where's Brita?" Ayesha looked at the men and then outside to see only Infected coming towards them.

"They got her," Tony said.

"Yeah," Matt nodded, "we have to fucking go."

Selena looked beyond the panting men towards the Infected that were within five feet of the car. She could do nothing but drive. The old farm turned business centre had a paved road leading off ahead. Not wanting to go back and face the Infected again she headed off this way, the Range Rover had four-wheeled drive anyway if they ran into trouble. The single lane was Infected and debris free and to her relief, it turned right and re-joined the lane leading back up to the farm. They were soon back where they had started, with no new supplies and one less group member.

Brita rushed through the ruins of the ground floor of the large house at the sound of the first car horn. Then up a confined winding servant's staircase, by the kitchens to the first floor. She managed to get to a west facing landing window just in time to see Tony and Matt get into the Range Rover and for it to speed off leaving her behind.

She banged a fist on the windowpane, but it was no use; the car with the rest of the scavenging group had driven off without her.

"Fucking men, why didn't you fucking die," she swore at the window in her native Danish. She raised the axe to rent her anger at the window but was stopped by the smashing of glass somewhere downstairs. Brita rubbed at her bald head and then froze, gripping the wooden handle of the axe tightly. She crept to the balcony overlooking the large central staircase leading down.

Brita held her breath and listened. Two more loud smashes of wood and glass came from down below and then the movement of many bodies below. She hurried back to the servant's staircase, hoping she had closed the door to it behind her, but she couldn't be sure. The stairs led up into the attic area. She could hear bare feet on the main staircase, so she ducked inside the servant's staircase, closing the door behind her and headed up to the attic area to see if there was anywhere to hole up.

She exited the tight round staircase into a small landing. The majority of the attic was open and full of junk, but two steps led up to a door. She followed that to find a maid or butler's room for when the house had been built. It was bare except for an old metal framed bed, and an old heavy wooden wardrobe. A skylight lent light from the rear of the property. Brita opened the wardrobe, but it was empty. She crept back to the doorway, only to hear the dreaded sound of many feet coming after her in pursuit. She closed the door. There was a large key in the lock, so she turned that giving her some protection. She turned and eyed the room. There was no escape for her. The Infected soon reached the locked door and began to pound on it and wanting her fresh uninfected blood. She tried to move the wardrobe, to block the door, but it was old and made from solid oak, and she could not even move it an inch. All she could do was to tip the bed over and ram that up against the door.

It might buy her some time, but it was hardly secure.

Brita raised the axe high above her head.

"I will be with you soon in oblivion my beautiful Ellie," she whispered.

Outside it began to snow again.

CHAPTER TWENTY-EIGHT

REVENGE

Hannah stood at the bedroom window looking out at the fast falling snow, a mug of lukewarm tea held between her cold hands. She could not quite believe that another of their ever-diminishing group was gone forever. She had on an overlarge pullover she found in a drawer, but still felt the cold through the back of her spine.

The others were downstairs discussing how the trip to the village had gone so terribly wrong so quickly. Hannah wasn't there, so had little to add, after she had heard all the facts. She missed Brita, she felt safe with her around. Tony and Matt did not give off the same vibe. Brita had hardly been their favourite person. Matt had used the situation to try and hug her, but she was having none of that crap. She was wise to his plans and ploys to get back into her good books and her knickers. If she ever wavered, she could just rub the small bump in her belly to remind herself how that had worked out before. She loved Ayesha and Selena, but with Brita gone Tony could play the Alpha-Male even more to dominate the group. Selena stood up to him but didn't have the aggressive thread that Brita had.

The snow had gone from a dusting to a foot deep quickly with the winds swirling around the little valley. She thought of her sister Hayley: she would have loved this weather. A tear rolled down her cheek and plopped into her drink before she could stop it. She drank her tea again, the tear for Hayley a reminder of whom she had lost. She watched the town below get covered with snow and as dusk approached, wondered if any Infected would make their way up the hill to the farm?

The light through the skylight was dimming and being covered with thick snow. The old sturdy attic bedroom door had held out against the Infected so far. Brita surmised that they might be good at biting and smashing through windows, but grabbing a doorknob with bloody skinless hands might prove a harder task.

The constant, almost wet sounding banging on the door was driving her to distraction, and she had a terrible urge to pee. Brita walked around the confines of the small servant's bedroom and flapped her arms to keep warm. At least she still had the axe, maybe she could cut up the wardrobe and start a little fire on the metal frame of the bed to keep warm. She knew it must be warmer in the house than outside, but it didn't feel much like it. At least she was used to the cold. The urge to pee overwhelmed her and having wet clothes when it was around zero degrees would not help her to survive this. She opened the wardrobe pulled down her jeans and underwear and peed inside quickly. She eyed the attic room door, hoping that the endless stream of urine would soon end.

It did, and with her heart beating ten to the dozen she pulled up her clothes quickly and closed most of her piss inside the wardrobe. She flexed her toes inside her socks and then continued her walk around the small bedroom. The Infected beat on the door harder. For both of them, it was going to be a long cold night.

"What if she escapes somehow and makes it back here, how do we explain that?" Matt asked in the pantry in an urgent whisper.

"Keep ya fucking voice down mate," Tony prodded him with a hard finger. "We keep guard each of us tonight. If she makes it back, then one of us shoots her with the old shotgun, claiming it was an accident, thinking she was one of those Skinners out there."

"I'm not sure I could just shoot her in cold blood."

"Really? Well, she left us for dead outside that fucking house and don't forget she turned your Ellie gay and cut you adrift in the Narrowboat too. If that hadn't happened, you would still have all the fingers on your left hand. Remember that, me old son. Now get out of my way I need a frigging beer."

Tony nearly bowled Matt over as he pushed past him. Matt winced at the pain in his left hand, thinking over all the things Brita had done to him. He just hoped the Infected had done the job for them, or they would have a lot of explaining to do. Tony took his beer back into the kitchen leaving Matt alone in the pantry.

Matt stared at the door to the cellar. He had killed for revenge before, he would just have to man up and do it again.

By three in the morning, Brita had had enough. She was getting stiff with the cold and was nodding on her shuffling feet. Even the Infected had seemed to grow listless outside the bedroom door. Desperate times called for even more drastic measures and freezing to death in a locked attic room was not the way she wanted to go out. She grabbed her axe and prepared for her do-or-die escape.

Ayesha was snoring loudly, and by four AM, Hannah had had enough. She had reached out to poke her friend, getting cold in the process, but the snoring hadn't ceased. Hannah dressed and pulled on her coat and boots and went over to the window to see how deep the snow was now. Even with socks on, her feet felt like ice inside her boots. She drew the curtain and looked down on the snowy land before her eyes. The glare of the white snow and a full moon made the night look as bright as darkness can be. The snow lay about a foot deep in places but had stopped falling from the sky.

She leant forwards and looked at the rear herb garden at the back of the farmhouse. As she was rubbing her palms together for warmth, something caught her eye. A set of single footprints broke the crisp snow, heading round to the back door. Hurrying past the sleeping Ayesha, she grabbed the shotgun her friend had brought up to bed with her to clean and rushed downstairs. She made it downstairs without tripping over her boots and into the kitchen. A lit oil lamp sat on the table, and a chair was pulled out from it, looking like someone had been sitting in it. A mug of tea was half drunk on the table. She touched it: it was still lukewarm.

Holding the shotgun, she moved to the back door to see snow and grey ice on the mat and two pairs of boots missing. Hannah found the back door was unlocked so opened it.

The snow around the doorstep had been heavily disturbed and dotted with drops of blood.

The set of tracks she had seen led round to the back door. To her right leading away from the farmhouse, up into the farm buildings were two overlapping sets of boots and double tram lines. Looking around the corner of the farmhouse she could see a light shining dimly from the office in the rear of the tiny farm shop, that she had never really explored. Two male shaped figures were dragging another unconscious looking person inside.

Hannah looked back into the semi-warm kitchen and wondered if she should wake Selena or Ayesha. But her curiosity got the better of her, and she pulled the back door shut and hurried along the tracks after the dark figures. Hannah was never a Girl Guide, but even with her limited tracking skills, the snow made the trail easy to follow. She followed the tracks around the corner of a dark building. Across the yard by the road entrance was the farm shop. The sliding door was slightly open still, and a dull glow shone from within. Glad of the snow to lessen the noise of her steps she approached the open doorway and peeked inside, shotgun barrel first. The shop smelt of rancid meat and all of the shelves it seemed had been emptied long before the group had turned up to claim the farm.

The light was coming from the open door of the office behind the counter. She could see movement inside and heard a ripping sound. Hannah gulped and took two steps inside the farm shop and froze. What remaining heat inside her body drained away through her boots and into the floor. She could see Tony ripping the underwear off the very pale behind of a woman thrown over the office desk. She could see the woman's trousers had been tugged down to her ankles. Her coat was still on, and she wasn't a conscious willing recipient of Tony's sexual advances. Hannah could not see her face until Tony pulled back from forcibly undressing her.

The victim was bald. The victim was bloodied around the head and obviously unconscious. The victim was Brita.

"So son, what hole you going for, the brown or the pink?" Tony said with a sneer, pulling up his own trousers.

"I'm not sure I can do it now," Matt whined moving into view.

Hannah stumbled back in shock at finding the father of her unborn child was party to the rape of one of their own. She stepped back and stumbled over a little tri-legged milking stool they sold in the shop. She fell backwards and fired once into the ceiling.

She managed to scramble to her feet up against a cold display unit when the two shocked men entered the shop. She gulped and raised the shotgun at them both.

"Well, looks like we have a problem here, doesn't it," Tony said menacingly, his shotgun pointing back at hers.

"Oh shit, oh shit, Han no, why are you out here?" Matt turned around once in shame, his good hand holding an electric lantern.

"Following a trail to two rapist cunts, it seems," she managed to croak back, her words were stronger than she felt at the moment.

"I never touched her, it was all his idea," Matt whined and pointed his good hand at Tony. Tony took one hand off the shotgun to whack his fist into Matt's nose breaking it with a crack and blood flew from his nostrils, sending the younger man to the floor in a sobbing heap.

Hannah should have shot him then when she had the chance, but fear crippled her.

"Look, Hannah, you're a smart girl, put down the shotgun and we can talk this over."

"You can't talk yourself out of rape you arrogant prick," she spat rage at the sight of Brita bare from the waist down and laid over the desk like a piece of meat.

"You don't know the circumstances luv. She was the one that cut the narrowboat adrift with Matt on board. She ran into a frigging house when we escaped the church, and locked us outside to die. This is just her punishment before we let her back into our cosy little family."

"Don't listen to him Hannah, he was going to kill her and bury her before anyone found out," Matt cried out, his mouth covered with blood from his badly broken nose. The lantern on its side next to the fallen teacher, casting eerie deep shadows across the shop.

"Got some balls now eh, have we? Well, I was going to kill her right away. It was old paedo teacher boyfriend here who had the idea of fucking her first, he wanted revenge for her dyking out his beloved Ellie, didn't he?" Tony said, in a stable menacing voice. He took a step towards Hannah, who raised the shotgun again.

"You're not going to shoot me Hannah, cos if you do you'll have to be quick before I give you both barrels to the old baby pouch area." Hannah couldn't resist a look down at her covered pregnant stomach area. It was enough for Tony; he lunged forwards and batted her shotgun out of her cold hands with ease. It went skidding across the floor and was stopped in the open doorway by the snow.

Hannah looked up in fright at the stock of Tony's shotgun as it smashed down on her forehead, sending her to the floor, the dark world going darker around the edges. She was bleeding, stunned with pain, but not unconscious. She looked up to see both barrels of the shotgun Tony was holding only eight centimetres from her nose.

"Sorry girl, you had to stick your beak in didn't you. Wrong place wrong time," Tony said with a cold level of disaffected malice that was a new low even for him. Hannah was holding her breath, she realised, so she gasped in air, knowing it might be her last breath. Then Matt jumped up, his face looking like one of the ruined Infected, with blood staining the gaps between his teeth. He grabbed the barrel of the shotgun and pulled it round away from the mother of his unborn child.

An explosion of light and sound echoed around in the small farm shop. Warm liquid splashed over Hannah's face. She saw Matt propelled backwards into a display case, which looked dark even in the semi-darkness of the farm shop. Matt let out a raging cry of pain and hopelessness and fell on his side panting in short bursts.

Tony turned the shotgun on her again. "Sorry, but it's your turn to die now."

Hannah looked over at Matt, who was a bleeding mess on

the floor also beside her. Through Tony's legs, she could see Brita was still lying unconscious over the desk in the office. Hannah closed her eyes and hoped that the pain of death wouldn't last more than a brief instant.

CHAPTER TWENTY-NINE

PUNISHMENT

"What the fuck are you doing Tony?" Ann shouted pointing the shotgun she had just picked up at her husband.

Tony and Hannah both turned to see Selena and Ayesha were standing behind Ann, and the snow had started to fall again behind them.

"Put the fucking gun down, Ann before you blow your own foot off, I've got this situation well under control." Tony barked at her without hardly a second glance.

"What have you done?" Ann asked again defiantly. The shotgun made her feel empowered and strong. The sight of Brita's half-naked form, Matt dying on the floor and her hearing her husband saying that he was going to kill an innocent pregnant girl made her question sticking with him all these years. Why she had put up with all his abuse for so long.

"I caught Matt raping Brita and Hannah holding her down as he did it. I intervened, okay. Now lower that shotgun and come stand beside me." This time, Tony did look at her, and she cowered inside knowing the wrath that he had meted out on her since their wedding day.

"That's bollocks, he raped Brita, Ann, and shot Matt and was going to kill me too," Hannah pleaded with her.

"She's right, Hannah wouldn't hurt a fly let alone do that," Ayesha said from the doorway, her numb hands gripping Piers' axe.

"Tony, we can all step back from this you know, sit down, work it all out," Selena said, trying to calm the situation down.

"Oh, shut the fuck up all of you, this has been coming for a long time. You fucking women and your talks and friendship and working shit out. That ends tonight, this is my farm now, and you all belong to me, I'm the fucking king here now, what I say goes. Now you can either join me and get in line or take your punishment like good girls." Tony boomed, spittle forming on his cold lips.

"You're insane!" Selena couldn't help herself.

Tony swung the shotgun up in her direction. He knew Hannah wasn't getting up off the floor anytime soon. "You want some then Judge?"

"What the fuck Tony?" Ayesha said in shock at the dramatic turn of events.

"You can stay, halfie, if you are good to me. Matt said you were pretty useful in the bedroom department. Ann get the fuck over here will you, stand by your husband."

"No," she shook her head.

"You promised to obey me, now get your fat arse over here, or I'll blow Hannah's head off, and it will all be your fault," he shouted at her.

Ann hesitated for a moment. She knew the force of his rages, but he had never had a shotgun before. He had beaten men half to death in fights, and her black and blue. With a shotgun in his mean fingers, she was scared that he would just kill poor Hannah where she lay. Ann gripped the shotgun hard and moved into the room. Now she could see Brita's pale abused behind and legs clearly, the blood on the floor from Matt's chest wound and the cut on the other side of Hannah's head. She stood next to him, but not with him.

"Good girl, now keep them covered," Tony nodded towards the open doorway.

Ann looked from the half-dazed Hannah to where Selena and Ayesha were standing. She had no choice but to do what he asked.

"What do we do now?" Ann asked him quietly.

"We teach these bitches to fucking respect me," Tony almost grunted sounding like a wild bull or hippo.

"And how do we do that?" Ann asked quietly.

"I kill either Hannah or Brita to show you cunts what happens if you defy me. And... cos you like chatting like little fucking sparrows so much, you bints can vote who gets to live and who gets to die."

"We can't do that," Selena blurted out.

"You fucking madman," Ayesha shouted at him, snow falling into her mouth.

"If you don't choose, I'll kill them both and then you'll be out of line and will suffer.

"So, Ann you are my queen in this new little kingdom of mine. So you get the honour of picking who dies first." He turned his crazy eyes on her.

"You," she simply replied and fired her shotgun into the trigger area of his weapon. It blew his right hand off. This rendered his shotgun useless as it dropped to the floor. Tony howled with rage, pain, and betrayal and charged at his wife. Using his good hand and bloody stump he charged her into a row of empty wooden shelving, knocking the wind out of her. His left hand around her throat squeezed hard and lifted her up off the floor as he choked the life out of her.

Tony suddenly stood up on his toes, all the air leaving his body. He looked at Ann, his eyes bulging like they might explode from their sockets. His hand tightened and her world went dark around the edges. Then he released her, and she slumped to the floor to see the handle of Ayesha's axe sticking out the back of his spine. He staggered back gasping for air, like a fish on dry land. To Ayesha's shock, he still had the strength to punch her in the mouth and knock her to the ground.

Selena charged at him and plunged a kitchen knife she had brought with her into his chest. Tony howled with pain, but still he would not go down. A backhanded slap knocked Selena into Ayesha as she tried to get up, knocking them both over.

"Is that it," Tony staggered round looking at all the women on the floor before him. "I'm your king!"

"And I'm a fucking queen," Brita said from behind him as she buried her wood axe into the top of his skull.

Tony staggered around to face her and then collapsed to his knees. With his dying strength he turned to look at Ann.

He even managed to raise his good hand towards her, before his damaged brain and wounded body finally realised he was dead. He fell to the floor at Brita's feet, as she struggled to hold her jeans up that had fallen back down to her hips. She spat on his back and buttoned them up.

Hannah fell sideward over to Matt as he looked at her with fear.

"Baby," he whispered through his chattering teeth.

"Yeah, our baby," she said and pulled him closer so his head could be next to his unborn child. One that he would never see born. He died there seventeen seconds later. Selena helped Ayesha to her feet and then went over to aid Ann. Ayesha looked solemnly at Brita and then gave Tony's corpse a hard kick.

Brita nodded back at her and did the same. Rubbing her throat Ann moved over and looked at Brita and Ayesha. They thought she might rebuke them, but instead, she kicked her husband's corpse in the groin. Selena followed suit and Ayesha and Brita helped Hannah up so she could aim a weak kick at Tony's nose.

Bleeding, the five women left the shop and helped each other back to the farm house.

CHAPTER THIRTY

WINTER

"How was it?" Hannah bent around from where she sat at the kitchen table, as the three women entered the house, sending a stream of cold air into the warm kitchen.

"Same as the village," Selena replied as she, Brita and Ayesha stamped the snow off their boots on the backdoor mat.

Brita was the first to slip her boots off and enter the kitchen still wearing her parka hood up. "The Infected we found were all dead, all frozen to death. Without their skin, this cold just kills them off fast."

"That's good news," Ann smiled and popped off Brita's hood to rub her stubbled head.

"Yes, but we couldn't get far in all this snow, we are pretty much cut off for the time being," Selena entered the kitchen now her coat was on its hook.

"Then we are safe here, for now?" Hannah said brightly.

"It seems so," Selena nodded.

"What happens if people, I mean healthy people turn up?"

"We defend what we have," Ayesha replied, the last to enter the room.

"That's not what I mean. What happens if the police or the authorities turn up, what do we say about how we survived or what happened here?" Hannah looked concerned; she did not want to give birth in jail.

"We lie," Ann said abruptly.

"Then we better practice our lie, until even our brains think it's the truth," Selena stated.

CHAPTER THIRTY-ONE

SPRING

Hannah was alone in the farmhouse when they came. Ayesha and Brita were in the far field, trying to work out how to plough the thing with the tractor. Selena and Ann were down in the village going from house to house looking for supplies not spoilt by the floods, mud, and hard winter.

She grabbed the shotgun by the back door, wishing she had more on than some old pyjama bottoms and a crop top that did not hide her expanding breasts too well. If she knew she would have company that early March morning, she would have dressed for the occasion. She might have put on some shoes and not the fluffy slippers she wore. The green truck had pulled up on the road and men were jumping out the back, armed men.

Hannah managed to open the back door and point the shotgun before the four men could raise theirs.

"That's far enough, what do you want?"

The Captain looked at the young pregnant girl holding the shotgun at him and raised his eyebrows under his beret. The extended belly was hard to miss as most of it was on show under her skimpy top. He had seen a lot of strange and terrible things since the floods and Red Death hit the UK, but this was right up there with them. "We are checking in this area for survivors, and it looks like we have found one. Do you want to lower the shotgun miss?"

"You the army then?" Hannah did not lower the shotgun.

"Yes," he nodded, raising his hands and taking a step forwards. "Are there any others here with you?" He resisted the urge to say 'grownups.' He tapped the clipboard under his left armpit nervously.

"There are five of us in total. What do you want here?"

"To rescue you or at least give you some supplies. Register you on the survival list of people and assets we are drawing up for this area. Can I have your name miss, age and where you were born and lived?"

"Who's drawing up?"

"The government. The crisis is over. The winter killed off the Infected and the infection. The power stations are slowly coming back on, and the water supply is clean to drink again. We have vaccines for the Red Death, and the floods threats are slowly diminishing. It's over. We can take you and anyone else to a hospital in Southampton to get vaccinated, and you could get your bump scanned." The Captain pointed to her belly and smiled.

"My name is Hannah Britton. I'm seventeen, and I was born in Chertsey and lived in Hersham in Surrey before the outbreak," she said and lowered the shotgun barrel.

"Long way from home," the captain said filling in a form on his clipboard. "You must have some tale to tell."

Hannah rubbed her belly and just nodded.

ACKNOWLEDGEMENTS

Books are written alone, but here are a few people I'd like to thank along the way on my journey from starting out to here. They have all helped shape my writing journey in one way or the other: Sarah Walker, Paul D.Voyce, Daniel Boucher, Rachelle Bronson, Dave Jeffery, Joe McKinney, David Moody, Adam Nevill, Johnny Mains, James Herbert, Len Maynard, Mick Simms, Mark West, Frazer Lee, Don D'Auria, Dean M. Drinkel, Helen Hopley, Martin Roberts, Stuart Young, Jan Edwards, Adrian Chamberlin, Stuart Hughes, Stephen Bacon, Richard Farren Barber, Peter Straub, Andrea Millard, Lisa Childs, Simon Clark, Samantha Lee Howe, David J. Howe, Mathew Riley, Steve Upham, Jeanna Gates, Bill Hussey, Garry Charles, & Jim McLeod.

With extra grateful thanks to the two Davids for making it this book and others happen.

ABOUT THE AUTHOR

Peter Mark May is the author of seven horror novels and one novella: *Demon, Kumiho, Inheritance* [P. M. May], *Dark Waters* (novella), *Hedge End, AZ: Anno Zombie, Something More Than Night* and *Forky's House.*

He's had short stories published in genre Canadian & US magazines and UK & US anthologies of horror such as *Creature Feature, Watch,* the British Fantasy Society's 40th Anniversary anthology *Full Fathom Forty, Alt-Zombie, Fogbound From 5, Nightfalls, Demons & Devilry, Miseria's Chorale, The Bestiarum Vocabulum, Phobophobias, Kneeling in the Silver Light, Demonology* and *Tales From the Lake Volume 5.*

He also writes historical crime under the name Alexander Arrowsmith. His first two of a series of novels, *The Athens Atrocities* and *The Medousa Murders,* were published in 2019.

He also runs Hersham Horror Books and has published twenty-eight books so far.

Website: http://petermarkmay.weebly.com/

www.ingramcontent.com/pod-product-compliance
Lightning Source LLC
Chambersburg PA
CBHW020408180626
46812CB00003B/883

Curious about other Crossroad Press books?
Stop by our site:
http://store.crossroadpress.com
We offer quality writing
in digital, audio, and print formats.